A

STUDENTS'

TREASURY

OF

TEXAS

POETRY

A STUDENTS' TREASURY OF TEXAS POETRY

Billy Bob Hill, *editor*

TCU PRESS   *Fort Worth, Texas*

Library of Congress Cataloging-in-Publication Data

A students' treasury of Texas poetry / Billy Bob Hill, editor.
p. cm. --
Includes index.
ISBN-13: 978-0-87565-353-2 (cloth : alk. paper)
ISBN-10: 0-87565-353-7
1. American poetry—Texas. 2. Texas--Poetry. I. Hill, Billy Bob.

PS558.T4S78 2007
811.008'09764—dc22
2007019312

TCU PRESS
P. O. Box 298300
Fort Worth, TX 76129
817.257.7822
http://www.prs.tcu.edu/
To order books: 800-826-8911

CONTENTS

To A.C. Greene

(1924-2002)

teacher and friend

INTRODUCTION

by Billy Bob Hill

ꙮ

THIS COLLECTION LOOKS AT MULTI-FACETED TEXAS as seen by Texas poets. *A Students' Treasury of Texas Poetry* is published as an interdisciplinary resource for Texas and American history teachers—and for English teachers who would find a place for Texas culture within their American literature curriculum.

Why did I compile *A Students' Treasury of Texas Poetry*? I would share what I know with my fellow teachers and with their students. To do so would be an honor, and I thank TCU Press for the opportunity.

I am a native, so I cannot recall where or when my fascination with the land and people of Texas began: in Big Bend setting up tents with my parents? In my seventh-grade history class where Miss McDade did her best to interest my class and me in Susanna Dickinson and Pecos Bill?

I know that I first understood poetry—in college. As a teenager, I didn't see the need for it. Fine by me if weird old William Wordsworth wanted to worship daffodils. Maybe folks in England did stuff like that. Middle and high school literature, poetry especially, seemed like material for somebody someplace else. In college, professors assigned poetry more within my experience, and from that point I grew.

Why use poetry to teach culture when shelf upon library shelf is stocked with award-winning prose?

I love a well-written biography, novel, play, or short story, yet poetry informs with a different emphasis and from a different perspective. Something in poetic mode helps readers remember content. If students fail to retain a fact or concept from traditional sources, I hope that teachers will give this alternative resource a try. These poems can be used for supplemental reading, extra credit, semester projects, and the like.

Of course, I did not think up the idea for inclusion of poetry into cultural teachings. Before Coronado survived the Panhandle, before Christopher Columbus or Leif Erickson landed, even before the first Americans trekked southward on the ice shelf, poetry was the official means by which language passed along history and cultural values. The tribes of the world expected their cultural stories to come with alliteration and a catchy beat. That was then.

Today, we read far more prose than poetry (when and if we read). Novels, creative nonfiction, and other varieties of prose are certainly worthy of their place in American letters. However, the ancient art of poetry can still tell what is important to a tribe.

Although I am a licensed, practicing instructor of literature, I struggle to explain to myself, much less to a roomful of disquiet college freshmen, why one poem succeeds while another one very much like it fails.

I see myself. The second class of the new semester has started, and I introduce poetry. On the board, I write the definitions of enjambment and allusion. My felt marker fades and I find another. I explain that allusions can knit poetry and history together. Now for the hard part. I list generalities about the essence of poetry. On the board, I quote Marianne Moore's definition: "Imaginary gardens with real toads in them." I see in my students' faces that the quotation didn't help. I copy an example of compressed language from my notes. The mini-unit is taking longer than expected, and I move along toward a pop quiz over a previous assignment. I admit that poems often treat abstractions (not bringing up Wordsworth's divinity in flowers)—while quickly adding that poetry, particularly narrative poetry, can deal fairly with tangibles while telling a good story.

The first chapter of *A Students' Treasury of Texas Poetry* offers narrative poems that feature a Texas hero, historical event, or cultural movement. These poems are designed to creatively enhance seventh-grade textbook content.

Anyone who knows Longfellow's line, "One if by land, and two if by sea," knows a part of the American Revolution. In varying degree, the poetry of the first chapter covers facts and concepts mandated by educational guidelines about Texas studies—with a dash of word magic and human drama thrown in.

The sixth chapter, "Lone Star People and Their Land," provides lessons about Texas sociology and geography. In other chapters, the poet's intent is more to convey an impression than directly teach a lesson. For some students, these impressions turn out to be what opens doors to further study.

How did I pick the poems in *A Students' Treasury of Texas Poetry*? I read old Texas collections; book publishing in Texas has a venerable history in itself. I tried to keep pace with all of our state's literary magazines. I attended public readings, and Texans sent me poems.

What kind of people wrote these poems? Something like two-thirds of contributors are or were faculty members of English Departments—that's how the majority of Texas writers manage to pay bills.

But thirty or so contributors work in nonacademic careers: I was a friend of this postal inspector, and there's a 9-1-1 call-taker, a computer analyst, and two poets in law enforcement, along with the others at their sundry days jobs

Laurence Chittenden, a best-selling poet, lived as a working cowboy. Red Steagall, a popular poet and songwriter, is a cowboy. One contributor to *A Students' Treasury of Texas Poetry* rode herd around Archer County as a teenager before becoming a poet, screenplay writer, novelist, who now, I suspect, has few problems paying bills. I could not fit in every type of Texan or every possible aspect of our culture into seven chapters, but one cannot say that this anthology under-represents the Texas cowboy.

Some from the past were hardly typical poets. Bonnie Parker wrote poetry in between reloading her guns. The two poet-statesmen, Samuel Houston and Mirabeau Buonaparte Lamar were also familiar with violence. I don't know if Lamar, the more prolific versifier, ever read a poem by Houston. If he did, I bet he hated it. History records that Lamar hated most everything about Houston and vice versa. I take pleasure in placing their works within a few pages of each other. I hope neither returns from the dead to express displeasure with my sequencing.

And I hope that teachers will use this book in their lesson plans and that students who do not like poetry will read a few of these poems and remember a line or two.

Billy Bob Hill, Ph.D., was publisher of Browder Springs Press and co-editor of the literary magazine, *iTex!* in addition to *Texas Short Fiction* and *Texas Short Fiction 2*. He also edited the anthologies, *Texas Short Stories* and *Texas Short Stories 2* as well as *Texas in Poetry* and *Texas in Poetry 2*. Hill teaches English in the Collin County Community College District.

CHAPTER ONE

PREHISTORY

INTO

PRESENT

CADDOAN INDIAN MOUND 1.
Larry D. Thomas

Near Crockett, Texas,
the wind, warm still
after all these years

with the chants of shamans,
whispers through the needles
of pines, and eddies

about the beaks of owls.
Tens of feet in height
it rises from the earth

in a breathless
ritual of moonglow,
this mound of pure spirit

Larry D. Thomas

ascending the night sky
on its staircase
of sacred skulls.

2004

THE WEEPERS 2.
Isabel Nathaniel

(In 1528 the shipwrecked Cabeza de Vaca and a dwindling number of armada survivors lived for a time with Indians who roamed the narrow islands of the Texas coast. His account describes their curious ritual of weeping, how as another culture might salute or bow or make the sign of the cross, these people wept.)

This is the island named Misfortune
where Karankawas are weeping
and the sea is wildly in agreement:
sorrow, sorrow.
         From the terrace
how white everything white is in the dark,
simplified and heightened:
parallel lines of waves fixed
as if by brush in titanium white
and the beach a long white stroke
to darkness.
         It would be the same
even then, this edge of the New World.
This sea over and over, this trek of moon.
The wind in this direction,
this smell of salt, of weather.
         And the weepers
starting up. A half hour of wails
for greeting. How are you? Not too good.
Simplified and heightened.
The castaways were impressed
with such lively sense of their own calamity.
To this island we gave the name Malhado.

Night makes dark mirrors of the terrace windows.
Inside I appear out there, come
so far, castaway from some
         old world.
The weepers are assembled, their lamentation
rising in this direction, profound, insistent,
all the years ahead
come to an end alike forlorn and fatal.

1996

CORONADO POINTS   3.
Alan Birkelbach

In Floyd County, near Floydada,
the man who lived in a nursing home
kept the chain link glove he had found over thirty years ago
in a box.

While probably important, he'd been told,
it didn't prove much of anything. It had less
conversational magnetism than a box of someone else's medals.
It was just something limp lying around.

It wasn't until folks starting finding
copper crossbow points in that same canyon
where the old man had wandered
that someone who knew someone

dropped off a letter to an anthropologist
who right off said, "Coronado. Yes, I'd bet,
by God, he passed this way looking for that place,
looking for Quivira,

where there were huge boats and monstrous fish
and 'las platas de oro.'" That anthropologist,
when he heard, had to wipe his mouth.
"You wait," he said,

"People will be digging there for years
looking for more proof, looking for the trail."
A scanning hawk, that far-off day,
might have seen the falling glove's glimmer

or maybe he flew on, intent on prey in
the next canyon, or maybe that glove fell
across the path of a route-ruled rattler
who, envious, of the fine scales, struck,

and then followed his natural track. Or maybe
someone should hurry back to that nursing home
in Floyd County, near Floydada, and find
that man who's still got the box,
and ask him quick, before he dies,

"Tell me,
when you first saw it lying there,
exactly which way
were the fingers pointing?"
1998

4.

MISSION SAN JOSÉ
Carmen Tafolla

The rocks are warm
have had the hands upon them
through the years
with sun to bake in
memories.
Gentle, even with
ungentle missions,
somehow life got through
to Them,
the priests amazed
that rabbit tasted
good,
slowed their passion fervor

one San Antonio sunny afternoon
learned to
lope
a bit
and breathe
with warm brown human flesh
touched the rocks in
tenderness
one time too many,
ceased to call it mission
as it grew to make itself
home
for all of us.
1992

TEXIAN CALL TO ARMS 5.

Sam Houston

Unfurl the banners to the breeze,
    Come rear the standard high:
Upon our mountains, shores and seas,
    Be liberty the cry.

Shout the glad word—and shout again,
    That makes each bosom swell.
Bid the drum beat a martial strain
    Bid it sound oppression's knell.

To arms! to arms! Let each firm hand
    Its battle sabre wield.
The oppressor comes—but stand;
    To tyrants never yield.

And bloody be his welcome here,
  Who would our sort enslave.
His myriad host we cannot fear:
  Who would? Tis not the brave.

On. On! and struggle to be free,
  And battle bravely on!
Our country calls—and who will see
  Her call in vain? Not one.

By our God—by our soil—we swear
  Freemen to live—or die.
And now 'tis done—the standard rear
  Be liberty the cry!

Shall these rich vales, these splendid pines
  E'er brook oppression's reign?
No! if the despot's iron hand,
  must here a scepter wave,
Raz'd be those glories from the land,
  And be the land—our grave.

1835

6.   THE WITNESS, SUSANNA DICKINSON

Violette Newton

March 6, 1836
They had chosen their deaths and martyrdom,
They had chosen to stay, and one by one,
I saw them fall—I can never erase
The sight of each bloody and broken face.

Still, through the years, I remember well
How I cowered there in the hours of hell,

For I was the only one left to say
What had happened there on that fateful day.

I was the one who must suffer the pain
Of the story I told again, again.
I was the one who could never forget
But must tell it over to all I met.

And I was the only one left to know
What we lost and gained at the Alamo.
1986

SAN JACINTO 7.
Mirabeau B. Lamar

Beautiful in death
      The soldier's corse appears,
Embalmed by fond affection's breath
      And bathed in his country's tears.

Lo, the battle forms
      Its terrible array,
Like clashing clouds in mountain storms
      That thunder on their way.

The rushing armies meet,
      And while they pour their breath,
The strong earth trembles at their feet,
      And day grows dim with death.

Now launch upon the foe
      The lightnings of your rage!
Strike the assailing tyrants low,
      The monsters of the age!

They yield! They break! They fly!
    The victory is won!
Pursue! They faint, they fall, they die!
    O stay! the work is done.

Mourn the death of those
    Who for their country die,
Sink on her bosom for repose
    And triumph where they lie.

Laurels for those who bled,
The living hero's due.
    But holier wreaths will crown the dead—
A grateful nation's love!
1836, 1902

8.   MIRABEAU B. LAMAR
A.L. Crouch

Mirabeau B.
(Buonaparte) Lamar
Hitched his wagon
To the Lone Star.

With a sword in one hand
And a pen in the other,
He earned almost
Enough glory to smother.

He wrote some verses
And kept a journal,
And jumped in ten days
From Private to Colonel.

When hot lead and cold steel
Determined our borders,
He and Sam Houston
Were giving the orders:

Imperial Texas,
Claimed Mirabeau,
Included all
of Mexico …

Not only that
(The man was terrific),
He dreamed of a Texas
That reached to the Pacific!
1945

THE PLEA OF TEXAS 9.
Mary Austin Holley

Admit us—we would deem it shame,
Of other lands such boon to claim,
     For we are free and proud.
But we a mother's love may seek,
And feel no blush upon our cheek,
     Before her to have bowed.

We are thy children; doubt it not—
We've proved our birth on many a spot
     Where cannon thunder pealed.
'Twas Saxon heart that dared the fight,
'Twas blood of yours that gave us might
     Upon Jacinto's field.

13

Rebels, they say! We learned from you
What freemen could and ought to do.
      Against a tyrant's might—
And what by valor first we gained,
And have for eight years full maintained,
      Is ours by every right.

They call us poor! 'Tis false—the Sun,
A fairer land never shone upon,
      Than this we offer you.
We are no beggars—well we know
The worth of what we would bestow—
      We have not gain in view.

We love your flag, your laws, your land—
Wishing to worship, see we stand
      At Freedom's Temple door.
Admit us now for it may be,
That tost on Time's tempestuous sea,
      We part to meet no more.

1844

10.   FOR MAXIMINO PALOMO

Teresa Palomo Acosta

the official history that
traces in pictures and words,
endlessly depicts
in minute detail
the stealing of your honor
the selling of your manly labor,
the pain you endured
as sons and daughters
drifted from you,

met their death in the
hour of thorns and swords
will fail you

just as will history texts
written with the cutting pen of
palefaced brown/stone men who recall 1848
and
forget to tell about
the man who cradled children to sleep,
soothed their damp hair,
told them stories,
played la golondrina on his violin,
and laughed
aloud
at dusk.

Teresa Palomo Acosta

*(The United States and Mexico signed the Treaty of Guadalupe Hidalgo in
1848, thus ending the Mexican-American War.)*
1984

TRAITOR   11.
(Sam Houston, 1857)
Pat Stodghill

He had been called many things by many men,
yet the word "traitor" went against the grain;
not when the new ones sneered,
but when old friends said it…
the ones who had been at Gonzales and San Jacinto,
who had voted to trade the single star for twenty-eight,
who now had changed their minds.
He spoke in cotton fields, corn fields,
on riverbanks and hillsides and on courthouse steps
saying, "We must stand by the Union."
They did not hear.

They did not want to hear,
puffed with pride and ambition, boasting
that no "northern states" could tell them what to do.
He warned of bloodshed, civil strife,
and they had laughed,
hurling epithets like stones around his head.
"So long as the flag waves over me,
I can forget that I am called a traitor," he declared,
remembering the sting of stone-tipped arrows,
the musket's ball.
What could the words do that the fire had not?
So he spoke on, ignoring crude remarks;
yet when alone, apart,
the word "traitor," loud as cymbals,
echoed in his heart.
1975

12. FAREWELL ODE TO SENATOR SAM HOUSTON

Jim Crack

Oh! Sammy Houston, now you'll die,
For "Cousin Muke" has raised the cry;
Your day is o'er, good bye! good bye!
     You're sure to go;
He'll learn you how to "nullify"
     'Gainst Mexico!

'Twas nought to you what Calhoun said—
Nullification laid him dead—
From Gadsden you had nought to dread,
     He spoke so blunt.

But now, alas! you're badly bled
             By Gen'ral Hunt.

No matter, Sam, 'tis your own chat,
Because he's great, don't lay him flat.
You say he's *whiggish, this,* and *that:*
             'Tis not the case;
He's proved himself a democrat,
             Here in this place.

He plainly shows he voted right,
Last for Taylor, first for White!
Oh! democrats, don't take a fright,—
             We'll all agree:
These votes alone prove to our sight
             Democracy!

Farewell, Old Sam, forevermore!
For you I grieve—my heart is sore.
You're gone—I'm sorry, but—'tis o'er.
             One thing I scan:
To die, it is an honor, sure,
             By such a man!

All Texas once obeyed your call;
Your race is run—'twas great and tall.
None, more than I, lament your fall—
             I'll mourn in black—
'Tis, though, the common fate of all!
             Your friend,
             JIM CRACK

1849

13.   TEXAS TRAILS
                     Norman H. Crowell

Trails that wander and writhe and bend—
Mighty trails…take them end to end.

Old trails made by conquistadors.
Trails to the far Pacific shores;

Gouged by the tires of the pioneers,
Cut by the hooves of the longhorn steers:

Devious trails where Comanches fled
On moonlit night when their hands were red;

Deep-cut trails through the gramma grass
Where the buffalo herds took a year to pass;

Trails on the sands where the buccaneers
Hid their spoils in the daring years;

Trails to the North where the cattle bawled,
Where the cowman bluffed and the gambler called;

Trails that saw brands on a heifer's hide
Still warm as the brander gasped and died;

Trails that knew the cow-puncher's tune
And the coyote's call to the thin grey moon;

Trails to the West where Kit Carson told
Of mountains laden with yellow gold;

Where long lean men spurred down the way
To the red saloons of Santa Fe;

West to the snowcaps through sand and mud—
A trail of battle...a trail of blood;

Where outlaws rustled and bandits killed
And the man who lived kept his right hand filled,

Down this grim trail tall wagons creaked
And stragglers died if their canteens leaked;

Here buckskinned scouts with tobaccoed lips
Slept by their fire of buffalo chips;

And the bullwhacker spat and cocked his eye
As the Pony Express went riding by;

Trails to the hills where the Indian fires
Told of the passing of their sires;

Winding trails to the mighty springs
Whose clear cold water forever sings;

Trails, criss-crossing, cutting deep
Where Texas heroes are at sleep;

Long trails writhing...trails that bend—
Mighty trails...take them end to end!

1937

14.   WAGONS AT DUSK
                      Grace Noll Crowell

Sometimes when the grass in Texas
Is deep and green and lush,
And the wind dies down at evening,
I can hear through the deepening hush
The sound of covered wagons
Creaking in box and spoke,
I can see them stop at nightfall,
I can smell the supper smoke.
And voices call through the darkness—
Lonely and strange they sound
In the vastness of the prairies
Between the sky and the ground.

And the ones who have chosen Texas
Because of its clean red loam,
Who are forging ahead to claim it
And name it for their home,
Dream awhile in the darkness:
An ancient wonder dream—
They see homes rise on the prairies,
See schools and churches gleam
Against the red of the sunset,
Against the rose of the dawn,
And, although their old homes call them,
Tomorrow they will move on.

1938

SITE OF THE INDIAN FIGHTS OF 1871, ABILENE

15.

Naomi Shihab Nye

little purple flowers under our feet

it's hard to imagine
the Indians finding one another
in this huge space
and having something to fight about

1973

MOONLIGHT

16.

Berta Hart Nance

My father hated moonlight,
And pulled the curtains down,
Each time the snows of moonlight
Came drifting on the town.
He was an old frontiersman,
And on their deadly raids,
Comanches rode by moonlight,
In stealthy cavalcades;

And took the settler's horses,
Or left a trail of red—
He came to love the darkness,
And hate the moon, he said.

1935

17.   BATTLE OF ADOBE WALLS

Chris Willerton

Headlong down the red dawn galloped
Lone Wolf, Quanah Parker, Stone Calf, White Shield,
three hundred Kiowa, Cheyenne, Comanche
flinging up dust and thunder, riding
red-eyed for scalps of buffalo hunters.
But the white men, warned early, fumbled for guns
in the gray light, yelled between buildings, above the boom
of a thousand hooves, black racket of war whoops,
gun butts battering the trading post doors.

Yet noon came, and nightfall, and corpse
after corpse. Ishatai's charm,
warpaint he said would turn bullets,
was a bad joke: the buffalo guns
spat death a half mile. Lone Wolf,
hair still docked to mourn his son,
watched other men's sons slung down to death.

The third day, squinting through the heat,
Billy Dixon even made sport. "A scratch shot, boys!
Them Indians are most of a mile away!"
Dixon's Sharps 50 flung slugs in a flat arc,
killed two hundred buffalo a week
but not at this range. Still,
when the rifle roared and they waited open-mouthed,
the bullet hit: a warrior jerked backward,
rolled off his horse, falling from the world.
He sopped the dirt red, his ears buzzing with death
and the white men's faint whoops and hurrahs.

The warriors who lived to be penned on the reservation
could tell their children, "The buffalo
would stretch to the edge of sky. Such a herd
took all day to run past." The buffalo were gone
in four years. Even the white men had to turn
barkeeps, marshals, ranchers,
staking the plains down with towns and fences.
Billy Dixon's widow last gazed at the land
from a motorcar.
1986

IN FIELDS OF BUFFALO   18.
Walter McDonald

Granddaddy waited while men with spades
dug a maze of trenches to test the treasure maps.
Skulls wedged up like onions on his farm.
Diggers from Austin brought along charts
of slaughter on the plains. By 1880,

buffalo hunters had aimed long rifles
where he plowed. Thousands dropped like manna
for horseflies, hides worth their weight
in silver in St. Louis....I remember the truck,
the loading ramp, crates of bones dollied aboard.

I hadn't known buffalo roamed there,
never dreamed his dirt was home to anyone
before Grandfather's father. Cotton
was all I'd seen on his rows, those skies
my only horizon. At night I listened hard

and heard far in the distance the howl of coyotes,
the thunder of summer storms. Lying still,
I felt an earthquake rumble, a herd
stampeded by rifles, miles of humpbacks
galloping, about to disappear.
1993

19.   CATTLE BRANDS
Vaida Stewart Montgomery

The pioneer artists had a canvas as wide
As the hairy surface of a steer's hide.

They worked with a red-hot saddle-ring,
An end-gate rod, or any old thing,

But they drew their lines and they curved them well,
From the Tumbling Crutch to the Dinner Bell.

∾

The Old Timer fumbled and muttered a damn
When they handed him an iron with a monogram.

"Just give me a gaucho, every time—
Them new-fangled curlicues ain't worth a dime."

The Old Timer's Brand was *I C U;*
The rustler changed it to *I C U 2.*

∾

The hard-riding cowhands played just as hard,
Nor batted an eye at the turn of a card.

There was a cowboy, Burk Burnett by name,
Who held four sixes in a poker game.

"I wager my ranch," the ranchman bawled—
He had three aces—and Burk said, "Called!"

So Burk won the ranch on a poker hand,
And henceforth used the *Four Six (6666)* brand.

∾

The pioneer women liked to see
The *Laurel Leaf* and the *Fleur de Lis*.

The pioneer men liked *Spade*, and *Star*,
Pig Pen, *Pitchfork*, and *Bar V Bar*;

Hog Eye, *Mule Shoe*, *Lazy J*,
Buzzard on a Rail, and *Anchor K*;

Buckle, *Broad Axe*, *Straddlebug*,
Bow and Arrow, and *Little Brown Jug*.

∾

The pioneer artists had a canvas as wide
As the hairy surface of a steer's hide;

And they drew their lines and they curved them true,
From the *Turkey Track* to the *Flying U*.
1946

THE JUDGE 20.
Claire Ottenstein-Ross

A lot of Texas tales are told
About old Judge Roy Bean,
Who was "Law West of the Pecos"—
A tough cowboy, lean and mean.

Claire Ottenstein-Ross

They say he came from San Antone
Where his customers got bilked.
He caused an awful lot of grief
Cause his cows gave funny milk.

The milk had minnows swimmin' in it,
So they ran him out that day.
He claimed the creek they drank from did it,
Then he made his get-a-way.

That's how he got to Langtry,
And with help from Texas Rangers,
He got elected as the judge
Even though he was a stranger.

Folks say he made up his own laws
And some were just for fun,
Like the time he fined one hundred bucks
To a corpse who had a gun.

He had a sense of humor
From the stories I hear told,
Like when he married folks he'd say,
"God have mercy on your soul."
Nobody ever questioned him
Cause they knew he wasn't foolin',
He'd shout them down and yell real loud,
"By gobs, that is my rulin'!"

So please don't doubt this Texas tale,
Or you'll give his corpse a nudge.
His voice will shout out from the grave,
"Don't argue with the Judge!"

1995

OLD FORT GRIFFIN 21.
Berta Hart Nance

Here once the endless wagon-trains
Brought hides of shaggy buffalo,
And brown adventurers raced by,
Trampling the April flower-snow.

Here once that columns hurried forth,
Against the steady southern gale,
Their guides, the friendly Tonkawas,
To find a red Comanche-trail.

The dove calls where the bugles sang,
The cactus-flower lifts a bell,
Where soldiers drilled, mesquites parade,
The mocking-bird is sentinel.
1931

HILL COUNTRY REST HOME 22.
Carol Coffee Reposa

At the fort the flag flies all night long.
Inside the cold stone rooms
Are broken lanterns
Gusts of wind, Comanche arrows
Memories of spurs and flint
Dingy photographs of Johnston, Thomas, Lee
Behind cracked glass.

From this rise a visitor sees everything:
The tired kaleidoscope
Of storefronts faced in river rock

Carol Coffee Reposa

Tile rooftops, stunted trees
And lines of slowly moving cars.

Beyond the hills
I hear the muffled roar of cannon,
Underbrush snapped
By rag-wrapped, bleeding feet
In quick retreat
A tattered blanket thrown across the back,
Dead dreams ripping at the brain.

Below are rusty pickups,
Tidy hospitals
Retirement homes to house the ghosts
Of other wars
While somewhere
Just before the morning medication
After all the doors are locked
The General surrenders
To the yuccas and bluebonnets,
While scores of wrinkled soldiers
Hobble on to Appomattox.
1983

23.   FOR ERWIN SMITH, COWBOY PHOTOGRAPHER

Larry McMurtry

Lead me along the hills,
    where naked young mesquites
Shiver in the twelve-day wind
        by stumps of burned ancestors;

Where the last badgers denned
    and yucca bloomed white
Among weed and thorn
    to the weedringed rocks
Where the bones are strown,
    white and dry on the dry ground—

Ribs, skulls, jaws
    with rotting teeth;
Bones of red heifers
    dead of a first bringing;
Bones of the early wounded
    Herd.

And here, the last cracked bones
    of my grandfather's horse,
The gray one who stood in grave
    infirmity under
Horsepasture elms through
    my boyhood.

An old horse, youth
    and the cantering after cattle
Lost, and lost calves,
    and myself, lost
To the white bones and the hills—
Busy with dove and rabbit,
    and the coyote tracks
Fresh every day in the creekbed
    mud—turning finally

Through your book
    and finding those grey doves
And tracks set back,
    the old bones sprung

Together and the unremembered
　　hills drawn into line.

You were, at the last,
　　as an old horse under elm,
Bending in pain to flavorless
　　grass, the dust taste
In your mouth—

You who in your youth
　　ranged the browning summertime
Canadian with a Kodak
　　and one pair of boots,

You and the onetime three-year-old
　　of the blurring dun
Legs, wonderers toward the end:

Was tobacco worth the walk
　　to store:
Could another winter
　　be endured?

Wondering, at the last,
　　if sinew had ever been strong,
If flesh and swift blood
　　had been real

If the wildtide Canadian
　　ever ran through such green range.

O pards, I hear the whistle,
　　but the train has gone.

1960

THE SIGH OF THE OLD CATTLEMAN 24.
Jas. D. Thorn

Oh, to close my desk, lay by my pen
And ride away to the range again;
The broad expanse where cattle roam
Where the great out-doors is home, sweet home.
The city's dust, the city's lust
That fills my soul with sheer disgust;
The lust for power, the lust for gold,
The lust for which our manhood's sold.
Oh, let me leave this hateful grind
And all for which it stands, behind;
The wicked city and its mart,
The seared of soul, the flinty heart.
To hear my pony's hoof-beats fall,
In answer to the wild bird's call—
The Texas plains once more to view
Where flowers flame—red, white and blue;
To lie at night, beneath the skies
That watch me with a million eyes;
To sleep, to dream and sweetly rest
Upon the friendly prairie's breast.
1931

A BALLAD FOR BILL PICKETT 25.
William D. Barney

Willie got born somewhere near Austin,
    a Texan as all agree.
He was some Black and some Creole
    and part of him Cherokee.

He learned to ride before he could walk
        leastways, that's as they say.
He'd stay in a saddle on a bucking bronc
        or out on the range all day.

He saw some cowboys branding calves;
        they couldn't catch the brutes.
Willie, he said, "I'll catch you a few,
        as sure as my feet is in boots."

They laughed at the skinny kid as he rode
        for a calf that was on the run;
he slid from his horse, grabbed the head,
        and down in the dirt they spun.

And the calf held taut. They still tell
        how Willie got him a grip,
for he held on to that yearling's head
        with his teeth in its upper lip.

"I seen a bulldog do that once,"
        said Willie when he was through.
"I says to myself, if a dog can do that,
        no reason I can't too."

His fame went through the cities around,
        how he could take down a steer,
grabbing its head and chewing its lip—
        he was a man without fear.

He even went down to Mexico City
        to work a wild bull in the ring.
If the crowd hadn't tossed brickbats,
        he'd have bulldogged the damn thing.

The Miller Brothers of 101 Ranch
     got word of Willie's fame.
Zack Miller, he came down to Cowtown
     to see him play his game.

There on the banks of Marine Creek
     Pickett bulldogged with a will.
Said Zack, "Join us, you're our man,
     and your name is henceforth Bill."

They held a big fair near Guthrie Town,
     the biggest ever seen
in the Territory, complete with horses,
     stagecoaches, a beauty queen,

Two hundred Indians from a dozen tribes,
     at their head Old Geronimo.
And cowboys by dozens and dignitaries—
     oh, it was a marvelous show!

But the biggest event of the whole day
     was bulldogging by our Bill.
He did himself proud, he showed them how
     and gave that crowd a true thrill.

He was with Millers the rest of his days,
     a showman they counted a friend.
When a wild horse kicked him in the head,
     Bill came to an untimely end.

And Old Zack Miller wrote a poem to say
     how "Old Bill is Dead" but still
would live on in the hearts of men.
     There's never be any like Bill.

On Exchange Avenue, North Fort Worth,
there's a sculpture of a brave man,
of a struggling steer got by the horns—
it's all to an artful plan.

Friends, honor the cowboy. Bill Pickett.
He was tough. He was good. He was game.
He fought with his hands, his heart, his teeth,
and he won himself a proud name.

1999

26.   GIRLS OF THE RODEO
Margie B. Boswell

Here come the dashing riders,
Girls who are Texas born,
Who know the rhythm of riding
Over prairie sage and thorn.

Watch how they cut and circle,
Canter and gallop and pace,
Each girl and horse united
In a flowing pulse of grace.

Surely such easy motion,
Free from strain and fear,
Comes only to those who are quickened
By the blood of the pioneer.

1949

THE GREAT STORM 27.
(multi-image documentary produced by C. Grant Mitchell)
Larry D. Thomas

The quavering words of those who survived
are voiced by sixteen actors
and overlaid with loud sound effects

and a stunning musical score
appropriate to the turn of the century culture.
Their sight barraged for a half hour

with brittle, Gulf-stained sepia photographs
and renderings of carnage
well beyond the feeble lens of a camera,

the visitors take deep breaths,
ease from the benches of the Pier 21 Theater,
file slowly out into the same

early September sun which finally
broke through the black-green storm clouds
one hundred years to the day before,

and head in their cars for the causeway
linking Galveston Island to the mainland
by the twisting, fraying skin of its teeth.

2002

28.   SPINDLETOP EVENINGS
                          Violette Newton

Listen, children, this was long before
anyone had TV or airconditioning, or at least,
long before anyone we knew had it. We used to go
over in that hour of the evening when fireflies
sparkled the grass, and we sat on Miss Kate's big
gallery in her wooden rocking chairs. Her gallery
rounded two sides of her house, and it seemed to hug
that tall structure in its loving arms.
It was high up, high off the ground,
not built flat on the earth
as your houses are.

We all got to rocking and talking events
of the day, but we knew our talk was a curtain-raiser
for the drama we always came to hear. So we bided time,
and after awhile, Miss Kate warmed up and started
talking of the long ago…before, during and after
Spindletop…the old days, the historical days
of our great event; and we lived those days
through her chuckling rememberings.

We buggy-rode in fancy to picnics out at the mound
where the odd smells smelled up the atmosphere,
and we curiositied as boys struck matches
to the crazy pools of ooze that oozed up
through the dirt, so fires danced everywhere
and lit up the place like a circus. It was
poor soil out there, said Miss Kate, unfit, really,
for rice, and unfit for cattle too. The grass.
wasn't good out there, it made the milk taste funny.

Miss Kate rocked us into Spindletop days
when the town went wild. Oh, we went with her
to the field to see what Mr. Trost took the picture of,
that black, gushing torrent pouring up the plain
white sky, and everyone getting spattered,
everyone screaming in a kind of insane joy,
some even rubbing the black stuff in their clothes
and skin. We stood amazed, like Miss Kate,
at grownup people acting like that. And she told
how the Crosby Hotel looked like the floor
of the New York Stock Exchange, with all
the buying and selling and wild speculation
and prices going up and down and Spindletop land
changing hands so many times a day that buyers
never even saw it. And she said anybody
with an extra room, or an extra cot, got rich,
selling sleep. And everybody laughed all the time,
even ones who couldn't understand why.

Violette Newton

Well, that was long ago when they had wooden sidewalks
built high above muddy Pearl Street, long before
they had great schools or a sympathy orchestra—
at least, that's what Miss Kate was apt to call it.
It was when the Lambs had the only piano in town
and it used to be carted on a wagon whenever
anyone needed it for musicals. It was long before
artists sat before easels in front of the few
old houses with tall, round towers in town,
young artists who wanted to preserve history,
and long before there was yellow smoke
going up from refineries, and black smoke
spewing from the bowels of millions of autos,
and black smoke belching out of airplanes overhead.

It was long before this, in our primeval,
uncivilized days, when it rained every day,
and there were many trees dripping rain,
and folks were mostly all poor
and wondering when and if the good times
would ever come.

We rocked into the dark
when the cool breezes started blowing
and bringing drifts of the Magnolia Refinery
and the Texas Gulf Sulphur to our noses. And when
we said, "Whew!" she admonished us, calling it
a right sweet smell, and for us never to deny it,
but take it in, take it in, it was our bread
and butter, it had put us on the map, it had made us
important enough in our country to be one
of the three strategic targets for an enemy
in case, and when, there ever was another
world dispute.

That was where the evenings ended
and we went home and got into beds
and lay there staring at the blackness
and slapping at the one flirtatious mosquito
who had followed us in. We lay staring
and wondering about things we couldn't put
our fingers on, things we couldn't even name.
We lay scared of we didn't know what, scared
and uneasy, with the lone insect sawing through
the darkness and the faraway hum of refineries
laving us to slumber in the sweat-dripping night.

1981

OIL WELL FIRE 29.
Grace Ross

Far off it is a rainy smudge against the sky;
Nearer, a storm-cloud in a fear-locked dream;
A mile away it is a volcano, savage and satanic.

The old woman on the hill says, "See,
The Devil has poked a hole through the ground—
Look at his black arm waving in the flame!"
1936

POEM TO MA FERGUSON 30.
Chuck Taylor

I've been sleeping out, Miriam,
sleeping out on county land,
working at getting the bucks together
to rent a place, and so public places
like our state capitol are good
for hanging out, passing time like
these old coots in Stetsons outside
on park benches, cracker barreling
wisdom even this late in the century—

So now I sit on a wooden chair
in the capitol rotunda, tourists
all around craning necks up,
up into blue dome—here I sit,
staring at your pleasant face,
Ma Ferguson, first oil portrait

to the right of south entrance.
Although your dress leaves shoulders
bare half covered by a shawl,
the artist hasn't painted you
Hollywood pretty. The chin is
solid, marked with a cleft; your
eyes are set in a serious thinking
frown; your cheeks, though rouged,
are firm. Miriam—Ma Ferguson—
Texas' first woman governor—
two terms yet. Two more
paintings down and there
you are again, older now, plumper,
flecks of gray in your hair,
grandmotherly, no shoulders bare.

Ma, you caught a lot of flak,
a lot of anti-feminist flak,
during both your terms of office;
some just didn't like it when
you said, "many women will be
invited to take an active part
in this administration." First
woman governor of Texas, from
a family with flash and flamboyance,
you passed a law that made it
a crime to wear the Klan's white
hood in public. Your daughter
says you were tough minded
—tough enough not to fear
advice from your husband
Governor Jim. A woman—you
know how they say—needs must
be twice as good as a man.

Ma Ferguson, Texas' first woman
governor, for a man like me, sleeping
out in my car in a camp like the
Hoovervilles of the Depression,
you mean something. A symbol. Right
or wrong, you and your husband gave
the impression of caring for
the little man. I remember you saved
a young Chicano from the electric
chair because it was his first offense.
You symbolized something here
in Texas, something we need to
keep in this greedy time when a
B-movie man strides this land
playing rhinestone cowboy, yes
you symbolized—shall I call it
the maternal? —love for the
family human, progressive populism.
1986

OUTLAWS 31.
Whitney Montgomery

Billy rode on a pinto horse—
    Billy The Kid, I mean—
And he met Clyde Barrow riding
    In a little gray machine.

Billy drew his bridle rein
    And Barrow stopped his car,
And the dead man talked to the living man
    Under the morning star.

Billy said to the Barrow boy,
    "Is this the way you ride,
In a car that does its ninety per,
    Machine guns at each side?

"I only had my pinto horse
    And my six-gun tried and true,
And I could shoot, but they got me at last,
    And some day they'll get you!

"For the men who live like you and me
    Are playing a losing game,
And the way we shoot, or the way we ride
    Is all about the same.

"And the like of us may never hope
    For death to set us free,
For the living are always after you
    And the dead are after me!"

Then out of the East arose the sound
    Of hoof-beats with the dawn,
And Billy pulled his rein, and said,
    "I must be moving on."

And out of the West came the glare of a light
    And the drone of a motor's song,
And Barrow set his foot on the gas
    And shouted back, "So long!"

So into the East Clyde Barrow rode,
    And Billy, into the West;
The living man who can know no peace,
    And the dead who can know no rest.

1934

THE STORY OF BONNIE AND CLYDE   32.
Bonnie Parker

You've read the story of Jesse James—
Of how he lived and died;
    If you still are in need
    of something to read,
Here's the story of Bonnie and Clyde.

Now Bonnie and Clyde are the Barrow gang,
I'm sure you all have read
    How they rob and steal
    And those who squeal,
Are usually found dying or dead.

There's lots of untruths to these write-ups;
They are not so ruthless as that;
    Their nature is raw;
    They hate all the law—
The stool-pigeons, spotters, and rats.

They call them as cold-blooded killers;
They say they are heartless and mean;
    But I say this with pride,
    That I once knew Clyde
When he was honest and upright and clean.

But the laws fooled around,
Kept taking him down,
And locking him up in a cell,
    Till he said to me,
    "I'll never be free,
So I'll meet a few of them in hell."

The road was so dimly lighted;
There were no highway signs to guide;
  But they made up their minds
  If all roads were blind,
They wouldn't give up till they died.

The road gets dimmer and dimmer;
Sometimes you can hardly see;
  But it's fight, man to man,
  And do all you can,
For they know they can never be free.

From heart-break some people have suffered;
From weariness some people have died;
  But take it all and all,
  Our troubles are small,
Till we get like Bonnie and Clyde.

If a policeman is killed in Dallas,
And they have no clew to guide;
  If they can't find a fiend,
  They just wipe their slate clean,
And hang it on Bonnie and Clyde.

There's two crimes committed in America
Not accredited to the Barrow mob;
  They had no hand
  In the kidnap demand,
Nor the Kansas City Depot job.

A newsboy once said to his buddy;
  "I wish old Clyde would get jumped;
  In these awful hard times
  We'd make a few dimes
If five or six cops would get bumped."

The police haven't got the report yet,
but Clyde called me up today;
  He said, "Don't start any fights—
  We aren't working nights—
We're joining the NRA."

From Irving to West Dallas viaduct
Is known as the Great Divide,
  Where the women are kin,
  And the men are men,
And they won't "stool" on Bonnie and Clyde.

If they try to act like citizens,
And rent them a nice little flat,
  About the third night
  They're invited to fight
by a sub-gun's rat-tat-tat.

They don't think they are too tough or desperate,
They know the law always wins;
  They've been shot at before,
  But they do not ignore
That death is the wages of sin.

Some day they'll go down together;
They'll bury them side by side;
  To a few it'll be grief—
  To the law a relief—
But it's death for Bonnie and Clyde.

1934

33.   BLACK SUNDAY, APRIL 14, 1935
("Dust Bowl Invades Texas" *Amarillo Globe News*)
Naomi Stroud Simmons

Naomi Stroud Simmons

April wind travels the snow geese route
south, south, south,
crossing borders, picking up cargo to be
delivered dark before dark.

April wind pushes prayers past store fronts
down side streets through church doors
where banked vigil lights bow in incensed
greeting as warm life invades cool pews.

We eat Mama's Sunday dinner with all the relish
of combines in summer fields while
April wind blows my empty swing
beckoning me for a free ride
winding, twisting, winding
as north horizons dull our sunny Sunday.

Soon Father calls me to the porch to face
the unknown rushing, roiling, rumbling,
swallowing the trees, the windmill, the barn.

We retreat, close the door, fall to our knees
and we are swallowed in darkness.

A drowning black sifts through our walls.

Fumbling for a small light that gives
candle power, Father casts us in sepia.

Wading through grit we seek dampened washcloths,
cover our faces, soothe our eyes,
breath dampness

while silent prayers have question marks.

1996

OUR CENTENNIAL! 34.

Preston P. Bateman

Our Centennial is a gala-day!
    Our Texas is a hundred years old!
Let's celebrate! Let's commemorate!
    Let's enjoy a thousand-fold!

1936

BALLAD OF A BOMBARDIER FROM TEXAS 35.

Goldie Capers Smith

Travis Brown saw the light of day
In a weathered cottage down Texas way;

His father chuckled and swelled with pride,
The happiest man on the prairie-side.

"Doc," he grinned, "here's my last red cent
Says you fetched us a future President."

Travis grew up astride of a pony,
Free as a norther, hating a phony,

As clean a guy as you'd ever meet,
Six-foot-three in his stocking feet.

Before he could blink he was overseas,
Wading in history up to his knees.

He wrote home, "Me and a guy from Dallas
Just went to tea at Buckingham Palace."

"The Queen, she passed us bread and jam;
I remembered my 'Please' and 'Thank-you-ma'am.'"

Then over the channel quick as a rocket
To drop a bomb in Hitler's pocket.

He pulled the lever for "Bombs away,"
Spit through his teeth and crooned this lay:

"We're over the top—so let 'em drop:
One for Mother and one for Pop;

"One for the Army, one for the Navy,
One for pork-chops, cornbread and gravy;

"One for the day when the war is over
And I'm back in Texas living in clover,

"Where a spade's a spade, and a man's a man,
And the prairie spreads like a palm-leaf fan.

"I'll marry a gal with a freckled face
And raise little dogies all over the place.

"We'll teach 'em to cuss and rope and ride,
to skin a steer and stretch its hide,

"To pass a football over the goal
For A&M in the Cotton Bowl.

"The world's too small—as you've got to know—
Hitler, for you and the *Alamo.*

"So junk your medals, and hold your hats:
The name of this ship is *"Rough-on-Rats."*

1944

COWGIRL   36.
Pat LittleDog

yes I was a cowgirl
living outside san antonio
on a military reservation
the year began with chinese fire
in korean skies
and you can bet I saw 7000
recruited young men
who moved into tents down the street
from my daddy-the-captain's quarters
january cold front and not enough supplies
my daddy said for so many men
not enough fuel for their tent fires and
from the school bus windows I watched them
swinging arms and legs together
calling out their rhymes
breath cold white

but fire of palominos
in the springtime
fiesta de los caballos
and you better believe I was a cowgirl
got the plastic yellow fringe
on snazzy vest and short-pants
my mama sewed for me
pre-pubescent vamp-of-texas style
(boots next year my daddy promised)
palominos lead all parades in san antonio
city of horses prancing
past ten-year-old cowgirls
lining the sidewalks
while someone is dreaming
of fire soon-to-be
in palomino stables
soon-to-consume palominos
too frenzied to gallop through flames
gala parade palominos

yes wasn't it only a dream
that fire would eat horses and men
up so soon?
burned horseflesh singed hair blowing
already through Gateway of Air
and all of its Forces
but I was only a cowgirl
yearning for boots next year
dreaming of creamy gold horses.

1985

THE EIGHTH ARMY AT THE CHONGCHON   37.
Rolando Hinojosa-Smith

Creating history (their very words)
by protecting the world from Communism. I suppose
One needs a pep talk now and then, but what
Gen. Walton H. (Johnny) Walker said
Was something else.

Rolando Hinojosa-Smith

Those were darker days, of course,
And the blinding march South
Cannot be believed
Unless you were there. But the point is
That the Chinese
Were stoppable, so Gen. Walker believed.

And he was right; later on he was killed
At one of the fronts, standing up
On a jeep. We understood.

This wasn't Ketch Ridge or Rumbough Hill
Or the Frisco-Rock Island RR Junction at Sill,
But then, it wasn't the Alamo either.

And those who survived
Remember what he said:
          "We should not assume that (the)
          Chinese Communists are committed in force.
          After all, a lot of Mexicans live in Texas."
And that from the Eighth Army Commanding
Himself. It was touching.
And yet, the 219th
Creating history by protecting the world from Communism,

Brought up the rear, protected the guns, continued the mission,
And many of us there
Were again reminded who we were
Thousands of miles from home.
1978

38.   REST DUE AND TAKEN
Rolando Hinojosa-Smith

General Walker is dead; killed in a road accident.
What a way to go.
No grudges about the Mexican crack;
We don't have to prove anything to anyone here.

I've not seen either Charlie or Joey since the Chongchon,
But we're all coming off the line soon.
1978

39.   THE CERTIFIED PUBLIC ACCOUNTANT
RECALLS THE EARLY 1950S
Robert A. Fink

We wouldn't have a T.V. set for years
and the picture show shut down on Sunday
in a town too private for a population sign.
Everybody went to church or sent regrets,
so after clearing off the table
and the regulation nap,
what was there to do but load the Ford
for a drive in the country?

Every road wore a number
Father, the mathematician, knew by heart
and recited like language
one enjoys against his teeth.
Mother sang the names of towns
(Smyrna, East Point, New Hope)
we could turn to in a jiffy.
Someone there was always distant kin.

Black Gum   Red Oak   Maple
Dogwood   Magnolia   Pine.
Father's pointing finger named each tree,
recounted the legend of its leaves
as if he hadn't changed the ending
so they all lived happily ever after
like the crows laughing
from the new-strung power lines;
the girl sitting on her Shetland pony,
not even casually interested in our passing;
and the pair of Snowy Egrets
lifting from a lily pond,
wings heavy as angels
charged with annunciation.
1989

Robert A. Fink

THE VISIT   40.
(from The Death in Our Family)
Gene Shuford

One can never tell what November will be in Texas:
it has that delusive warmth of the blood and love,
promising tenderness forever as though death
will never come: it will let lilacs bloom

in the autumn and the great sun shine with a burning
that invites the ultimate passion for living even
while the frost waits in tonight's sleep.
The rain can fall in the night and the sky will wash blue
as a baby's eyes in the morning and the puddles will dry
and the big jet will slip down out of cottony clouds
and the prince and the princess descend and all the banners
will wave above the spirit's shining armor.
Already this is a legend, a myth we only half believe,
saying, surely it must not have happened; surely, it must
have been a dream; surely, it was long ago,
but now is already encrusted with myth and the passion
for forgetting, strong as the passion for remembering,
so that both have woven a golden cloth for the years
of Camelot that were ours, for the greener fields that were ours,
for the tall castle we saw in the clouds, for the knight
and his lady dropped down from the sky who were our king
and the fairest queen we had ever seen walk proudly
across the tapestry of our time, which before
this day was done, all bloody on the stones
would lie and trampled with the blackest death
a man would ever see or bear to dream of.
1965

41.   WAITING WIFE

Marcella Siegel

She sped the daytime hours
in a coffee shop on Powell Street
where commuters, tourists and shoppers
streamed in from the cable cars
to have her serve their hurry.
Nights in her flat in an old skinny house
she wrote him letters

that smiled at how the flower stalls
splashed spring on the downtown winter;
how a rock out in the bay
blossomed sometimes like an April tree
with the satin bodies of seals;
and how a rat she had christened Ben
was her kitchen companion at night.
And she was careful not to tell him how alone she was
listening to young laughter passing by on the sidewalk
outside her window
in that city so alien to her East Texas town,
that city by the sea
where she had come, to feel closer to him
while she waited for his return.
She read in his letters of the refugees
on the road from An Loc
turning their tired backs on their smoking huts,
of the old young mothers and their wasting children
walking the napalmed fields,
and of his buddy stilled in the mud at Quang Nghai.
And she wondered when he lay in a steaming paddy
waiting for a shadow to move or explode
if her love beside him
would be enough.
1973

Marcella Siegel

TEXAS: SESQUICENTENNIAL   42.
William V. Davis

The Indians found the best places
first. They had everything
they needed: water, fertile soil,
good hunting. Forget the sun
all summer, forget the white men,

coming from the east,
the dark men coming from the south,
the buffalo moving west.

Before long, all the Indians
were gone: driven off, dead, caught
and kept in designated areas
nobody else needed, just then.
Cattle, cotton, the oil,
were the only money. Everything
went west. When enough wagons
broke down, they founded a town
and started to brag on it.

A century and a half later,
nothing's changed. The movies
have arrived. The latest news gets through,
eventually. But the land hasn't forgotten.
It's taking its revenge,
acre by acre, mile by mile, above
and below. The settlers, though,
continue to circle their wagons,
continue to stand and fight,
against the enormous odds.
1986

43. RIDDLES COME CLEAR AT MIDNIGHT
Walter McDonald

A car honks at midnight. I'm at the pond,
snapping twigs into pieces and flipping.
Maybe coyotes crossing the road,

four eyes in the edge of the headlights,
the driver thinking he's found teenagers
down on a blanket. It isn't a pickup,

silent until a whine of tires goes by.
Old friends come suddenly back
like that. A jolt in the brain

and Kelly's here, like Van Heflin with wings,
wide Irish smile, flying an F-4 fighter
south of Da Nang. Most months

Walter McDonald

I can't believe he vanished at 10,000′,
that he's gone. They think his bombs
exploded when he touched the button,
wired by a nineteen-year-old mechanic,
or a missile hit the bomb rack
at that second. Fate, unstable as air,

changed Kelly to heaven, sudden as a horn
I believe when I hear it, a shock
before fast-spinning tires.
2005

EXHAUSTED BY I-35, A COUPLE COMES UP ON THE THIRD BELTON-TEMPLE EXIT

44.

Lewis Salinas

Please, please, mi querida,
   Please, remember how you get the blues,
   Every time, every time, you listen to the news.

Just look. There. Springtime.
Bluebonnets bloom, bumblebees, buzz,
   and these NAFTA truckers will kill us before Al-Qaeda does.

Enough with the radio.
Oh, please, Sara, don't be sad.
Only find the iPod and go back to good moments that we've had.
2005

45.   FATHERS AND SONS
Walter McDonald

I rattle the porch as I walk, closing the screen door softly,
guided by the coffee pot's red light. Quietly,
I fill the china cup, a gift from my wife, still sleeping.
Four, no, five A. M., the clock's red digits say. Pace if I must,
but on the porch, far enough away from the bedroom

so I won't wake her, if I don't knock the cup off,
hunched at the screen still blue, waiting like me
for words that shoved me out of bed at three. Outside,
I hear crickets as if there's not a screen between us.
Cicadas have been quiet for hours, no barking dogs,

no trucks on the highway miles away, or I can't hear them.
I haven't heard a coyote since midnight, no owls,
nothing but crickets and the computer's hum, and this porch
that creaks and rattles when I pace, thinking of something
to write our oldest son overseas, a rapid force of soldiers

in the hills of Bosnia. In Desert Storm, he was out of touch
for weeks when nothing, not even a phone call or a fax,
could find him. My father died in battle so his sons

would never fight, far off on Guam and Saipan,
island hopping with MacArthur. Where I went is a footnote

in history books, stacks of facts we compiled about a war
already being lost, stored in a vault in Saigon
until someone shredded and burned them, pulling out.
I see blurred silhouettes of trees in the east.
I write about those trees, the crickets. I make up jets

overhead, letting down from Dallas. I lie about coyotes,
claiming they're back, howling the way our boy heard them
in these fields a thousand times. I say his mother's up,
here on the porch, sipping her second cup. I say
she sends her love, which is no lie. I say she'll write

tomorrow. I ask *How are you,* but delete that,
add something about the crops, the herd bull's shoulder
he hurt butting the barn. I go back inside for a cup,
and pace the porch until the sun is up. I close
with *Love,* and sign it, all my hand can do.

1998

CHAPTER TWO

All about Two Hundred and Thirty-Four Counties, the Art of Poetry Abounds

TEXAS POETS   46.

Boyce House

You write about bluebonnets —
In a land that knew Houston, hero fit for a Greek tragedy;
And about cottages nestling in honeysuckle —
Though there is the spot that saw Goliad's massacre;
And about white poplars marching up a hill into the sunset —
When men and women face the drouth, the sand, the wind —
and somehow smile!

Texas!
With its pirates' gold, its cattle-trails, its gun-fighters;
Its cotton fields, corn fields, wheat fields and oil fields;
Its lonely canyons, carved by nature, in a forgotten land,
Newsboys waving "extras,"
Wrestlers throwing each other out of rings while pale–
countenanced clerks shriek,
Clyde and Bonnie with blazing machine guns,
Farmer Jim and Ma Ferguson,
And seven million others doing things, brave, foolish, amusing
or what-have-you!
And yet, Texas poets, you swoon when you behold a dew–
drop enfolded by a rose!

1949

47.   HAIKU: HANDS SHADING MY EYES
Michael A. Moore

Hands shading my eyes
looking for a Texas cloud
to eclipse the heat.

2007

Michael A. Moore

48.   TEXAS TANKA
Robert Phillips

Winter storm warnings.
Deep snow in Amarillo.
Wrecks on icy roads.
Airline passengers stranded.
(Yellow willows in the snow.)

2007

Robert Phillips

SUNSET ALONG U.S. HIGHWAY 90 BETWEEN LANGTRY AND SANDERSON

49.

David C. Yates

Imagine a long brown poem—
As brown and as long as you can
Stretch it beneath a blazing sun
That melts your meters and leaves them

Broken and cracked upon the sand.
Omit all imagery and leave
Nothing to stretch for tension, nothing
To glue any adjectives to,

Nothing but an ocean of dull
Brown lines and an unbroken rhyme
That rhymes the same line after line
Far, far into the horizon.

David C. Yates

Now, draw a line down the middle
Of your poem for a highway
And wait, just wait for that blazing
Sun to fall and hug the horizon.
1979

THE EXPERTS

50.

Jack Myers

When the man in the window seat
flying next to me
asks who I am
and I tell him I'm a poet,
he turns embarrassed toward the sun.

The woman on the other side of me
pipes up she's four-foot-ten and is going to sue
whoever made these seats.

And so it is I'm reminded how I wish I were
one of the aesthetes
floating down double-lit canals
of quiet listening, the ones
who come to know something as
mysterious and useless
as when a tree had decided to sleep.

You would think for them
pain lights up the edges of everything,
burns right through the center of every leaf,
but I've seen them strolling around,
their faces glistening with the sort of peace
only sleep can polish babies with.

And so when a waitress in San Antonio
asks me what I do, and I think
how the one small thing I've learned
seems more complex the more I think of it,
how the joys of it have overpowered me
long after I don't understand,

I tell her "Corned beef on rye, a side of salad,
hold the pickle, I'm a poet," and she stops to talk
about her little son who, she says, can hurt himself
even when he's sitting still. I tell her
there's a poem in that, and she repeats
"Hold the pickle, I'm a poet,"
then looks at me and says, "I know."

1993

TEXAS POETRY   51.
Violette Newton

Up East, they do not think much
of Texas poetry. They think Texans
have no soul for aesthetics, that all
they do is pound their own chests,
talk loud and make money.
But every time I'm nearing Austin,
I look up at a painted sign
high on the side of the highway
that says, "Bert's Dirts"
and to pyramids of many-colored soils
sold by Bert, and I swell with pride
at that rhyming sign, I puff up
and point to that terse little title
and wish we could stop
so I could go in
and purchase
a spondee of sand
to make a gesture of my support
for poetry in Texas.

1981

THE POET GETS DROWSY ON THE ROAD   52.
Frederick Turner

He pulls off into the picnic area,
rolls down the seat, and goes to sleep.
An unkempt fifty-six-old transient
with a strong body, aching joints,
the sleep-narcosis of incontinence:

a possible problem for the Highway Patrol.
Over his dreaming head
pass the immense skies of Texas,
the roar and rush and whine of the interstate
and the remembered images of a life.

2000

FAMILY, FAMILY— IT'S ALWAYS FAMILY

THIS RIVER HERE   53.
Carmen Tafolla

This river here
is full of me and mine.
This river here
is full of you and yours.

Right here
(or maybe a little farther down)
My great-grandmother washed the dirt
out of her family's clothes,
soaking them, scrubbing them,
bringing them up
clean.

Right here
(or maybe a little farther down)
My grampa washed the sins
out of his congregation's souls,
baptizing them, scrubbing them,
bringing them up
clean.

Right here
(or maybe a little farther down)
My great-great grandma froze with fear
as she glimpsed
between the lean, dark trees
a lean, dark Indian peering at her.
She ran home screaming, "Ay, los indios!
A'i vienen los i-i-indios!!"
as he threw pebbles at her.
Till one day she got mad

and stayed
and threw pebbles
right back at him!

After they got married,
they built their house right here
(or maybe a little farther down.)

Right here,
my father gathered
mesquite beans and wild berries
working with a passion
during the depression.
His eager sweat poured off
and mixed so easily
with the water of this river here.

Right here,
my mother cried in silence,
so far from her home,
sitting with her one brown suitcase,
a traveled trunk packed full with blessings,
and rolling tears of loneliness and longing
which mixed (again so easily)
with the currents of this river here.

Right here we'd pour out picnics,
and childhood's blood from
dirty scrapes on dirty knees,
and every generation's first-hand stories
of the weeping lady La Llorona,
haunting the river every night,
crying "Ayyy, mis hi-i-i-ijos!"
(It happened right here!)
The fear dripped off our skin

and the blood dripped off our scrapes
and they mixed with the river water,
Right here.

Right here,
the stories and the stillness
of those gone before us
haunt us still,
now grown, our scrapes in different places,
the voices of those now dead
quieter,
but not too far away . . .

Right here we were married,
you and I,
and the music filled the air,
danced in,
dipped in,
mixed in
with the river water.
. . . dirt and sins,
fear and anger,
sweat and tears,
love and music,
Blood.
And memories . . .

It was right here!

And right here we stand,
washing clean our memories,
baptizing our hearts,
gathering past and present,
dancing to the flow
we find

right here
or maybe—
a little farther
down.

2000

54.   PRESENT MOMENTS
                 Njoki McElroy

I started the day with a jog/fast walk
Into crisp fresh air. Breath exhausting
Past present future terrors. Cooling down
With rhythms of Tai Chi
I know this won't be always.

AFTERNOON

Creamed the butter and brown sugar by hand
Saved some of the crumbly mix to top the batter
Two well beaten eggs and buttermilk with dissolved
Baking powder turns the crumbly mix to rich brown batter
Cinnamon, nutmeg, ginger, vanilla go in last
In the oven the spicy aroma seeps out and into my pores
Light like cake and spicy Perfecto
It is my Xmas gift to Cousin Twoshoe.

At her house she savors
The warm morsels and says:
Oh how did you know I've had a taste for Gingerbread?
She's my grandmother's first cousin
And at 103 (she says she's 111) is my
Last contact to my maternal ancestor's memories.

I'm not bragging, Cousin Twoshoe confides
But God has led me on a wonderful journey
And when He comes for me, I'm ready.
Granny Marinda (Let's see, she's your great great great)
Was 110 when He came for her.

I was a little tot when she came to live with us
But I never forgot my little dark brown
Granny dressed in a long dress, starched apron, bonnet
High button shoes, smoking a pipe, sightless eyes searching
A distant past, talking about slavery.

Dear Granny was sold several times.
She was a troublesome Runagate, always running
Running to find her freedom
Climbing trees to escape her captors.

EVENING

Green apples in Mom's red glass bowl, evergreen
Wreaths, Kwanza candles, spicy scents fill the room
My main squeeze pedicures my tired feet with patience
And happy-to-pleaseness. He pats my legs and says:
O.K. Cleopatra?
I smile and run my fingers through his soft beard
My feet are smooth
My soul is rejuvenated I'm ready to dance all night
I know this won't be always.

Njoki McElroy

NIGHT

At the party John Nickels and the Five Pennies
Play Blues, Country, Xmas
I don't want to make the gods jealous
But in my long flared red form fitting dress

I flaunt my good fortune
When the party ends, a stranger says:
Such a handsome couple—The two of you dance so beautifully.
I've lived this day of Present Moments well
If only this could be always.

2002

55.

THE MEMORIES IN GRANDMOTHER'S TRUNK
Red Steagall

Red Steagall

They came in a wagon from St. Jo, Missouri.
Grandmother was seven years old.
I remember she said she walked most of the way
Through the rain, and the mud and the cold.

She saw the Comanche, they came into camp—
Not the savage she'd seen in her dreams.
They were ragged and pitiful, hungry, and cold
Begging for salt pork and beans.

They staked out a claim at the cross timbers breaks
Where the big herds went north to the rail.
One day a cowpuncher gave her a calf
Too young to survive on the trail.

Their Jersey cow gave more milk than they needed
The calf grew up healthy and strong.
She staked him that fall in the grass by the creek
And pampered him all winter long.
In April her daddy rode into Fort Worth
With her calf on the end of his rope.

He traded her prize for a red cedar trunk
That she filled full of memories and hope.

I found grandmother's trunk hidden under a bed
In a back room where she used to sleep.
I've spent the whole morning reliving her youth
Through the trinkets that she fought to keep.

There's the old family Bible, yellowed and worn
On the first page was her family tree.
She'd traced it clear back to the New England coast
And the last entry she made was me.

I unfolded a beautiful star pattern quilt
In the corner she cross-stitched her name.
I wonder how many children it kept safe and warm
From the cold of the West Texas plain.

There's a tattered old picture that says "Mom, I Love You"
Tho' faded, there's a young soldier's face.
And a medal of honor the government sent
When he died in a faraway place.

A cradleboard covered with porcupine quills
Traded for salt pork and beans,
Was laying on top of a ribbon that read
Foard County Rodeo Queen.

Dried flowers pressed in a book full of poems
A card with this message engraved,
To my darlin' wife on our 25th year
And some old stamps my grandfather saved.

Of course there are pictures of her daddy's folks
They sure did look proper and prim.

I reckon if they were to come back to life
We'd look just as funny to them.

Grandmother's life seemed so simple and slow
But the world started changin' too soon.
She heard the first radio, saw the first car,
And lived to see men on the moon.

Life on this planet is still marching on
And I hope that my grandchildren see,
My side of life through the trinkets I've saved
The way grandmother's trunk does for me.

1993

56. OPPA

Jim Linebarger

You lived in hardy commonness: the feel
of gritty linoleum, the smell of snuff,
the cornbread and beans and onions you preferred
for diet, a faulty hearing aid, a ball
of string, assorted buttons, an embossed
red-letter Bible, dearly paid for with dimes
and pennies from a knotted handkerchief.

But miracles attended you as well.
My father laughs and swears he sweated dust
in the creaking wagon that you drove across
the Llano Estacado, but raised his eyes
to marvel at peaks topped with a white glaze
of winter. From your swept yard, behind a piece
of smoked glass, I saw an invisible moon
black out the sun. A patchwork quilt became,

under the light of kerosene lamps, a rose
window as we giggled and hid from the tame
and moral beasts of your imagination.
Closer to death, when your laboring tears
would gather to tell us of a new sensation,
your face was like a baby's taking love.

The ways of living are as various
as those of dying, but I fear them all.
Teach me your secret way for the dark times,
something to live by, perhaps a single word,
some kind of myth for your inheritors
who have no understanding with the sun.

1969

MI TÍA SOFÍA   57.
Carmen Tafolla

Mi Tía Sofía
sang the blues
at "A" Record Shop
on the west side of downtown,
across from Solo-Serve's
Thursday coupon specials
she never missed
—"Cuatro yardas de floral print cottons por solo eighty-nine
cents—fíjate nomàs, Sara, you'll never get it at that price
anywhere else!" she says to her younger sister.
And "A" Record Shop
grows up the walls around her like vines
like the flowers and weeds and everything in her
green-thumb garden
But here—

Carmen Tafolla

instead of cilantro and rosas
and Príncipe Dormido—
it's a hundred odd and only 45s
10 years too late
that'll never be sold
even after she dies
and a dozen hit albums that crawl up the wall,
smiling cool pachuco-young Sonny and the Sunglo's,
The Latin Breed, Flaco Jimenez, Toby Torres,
and the Royal Jesters.
Also: Little Stevie Wonder.
And The Supremes.
She sings to pass the time
"Ah foun' mah three-uhl
own Blueberry Hee-uhl."
She also likes "Lavender Blue."
It seems to be her color,
but bright—in a big-flowered cotton print
(from Solo-Serve).
Tía Sofía speaks Tex-Mex
with Black English
and all the latest slang.
Not like the other aunts—
Tía Ester, always at home,
haciendo caldo
haciendo guiso,
haciendo tortillas,
she never left the house
except to go to church,
braided her hair on top of her head
and always said
"Todos los gringos se parecen."
(All Anglos look alike.)
or Tía Anita—always teaching,
smart, proper, decent,

Tía Sara, Tía Eloisa, Tía Febe—
all in church, always in church.
Sofía said, "Well, I play
Tennessee Ernie Ford and Mahalia Jackson
on Sunday mornings."
And she did,
and sang along,
never learning that only singing in church
"counted."
She never made it through school either.
Instead of Polish jokes,
the family told Sofía jokes:
"Remember that time at the lake, con Sofía?
—Sophie! Come out of the water! It's raining!
—No, me mojo! (I'll get wet!)"
Always a little embarrassed by her lack of wisdom,
lack of piety.
After she died, they didn't know what to say.
Didn't feel quite right saying
"She's always been a good Christian."
So they praised the way
"siempre se arreglaba la cara,"
"se cuidaba,"
and the way she never "fooled around"
even though she could've
after Uncle Raymond died,
When she was still young.
(Only 71).

Funeral comes every 2 years in the family now
—just like the births did
60 to 80 years ago.
I remember a picture of a young flapper
with large eyes—Tía Sofía.
Between the tears

we bump into the coffin by accident,
and get scared
and start laughing.
It seems appropriate.
I also feel like singing
in a Black Tex-Mex
"Blueberry Hee-uhl."

1983

58. MY THREE UNCLES
Lewis Salinas

After my mother died,
  I had three uncles who would help my father as they could.

Uncle Jimmy Winston, my father's brother in-law,
  easy-going Jimmy, who looked like Mom,
  and Tío Alberto Pefialosa, his stepbrother,
  and Uncle Johnny Salinas, my father's true-bro,
  although he didn't much look like Dad.

Although they never showed up together,
  the three did separately drop by for a couple of Thanksgiving dinners in
Oak Cliff,
  which my poor father always cooked badly,
  but that's another story.

Uncle Johnny to Tío Alberto sometimes called out "Beto,"
  something that caused the younger man to grimace.
Jimmy, on the sofa, finishing off the mixed nuts,
  kidded Johnny about his leisure suit.

These three guys then pushing sixty always got along
  except that one Thanksgiving when the game against the Lions was on,
  they came close to an argument about how Coach Landry had been fired.

I learned from each,
  motorcycles, the Mexican Revolution, *Mad Magazine*, and so on.
I learned how three grown men,
  if from two or three unlike backgrounds,
  can manage to sit around a TV set and watch the same ballgame.

2004

TIA MARIA 59.

Teresa Palomo Acosta

The family has tried to say that her life followed a
singular path. Asi que de Tia Maria
many stories about her working very hard abound.
Especially about the many brooms she wore out sweeping
the Moody, Texas, post office floor.

But on a trip to her home many years later,
I glimpsed a framed deshilado that
she and 'buela Felipa had made.
Its intricately pulled threads
along the length of a cloth
told another story about her.
Julio, her eldest son, had rescued it from her trunk,
had it framed and hung on one of her living room walls.

I know that she and 'buela Felipa must have made it
during moments stolen for Mexicana painting.
Minutes taken mainly at night
after twelve daily hours of hauling and pulling,

of ironing and laundering—and cooking.
Only then, when no one was looking,
Tia Maria hizo su crochet, her needles clicking,
her body bent forward,
a shadow against the lamp.
She never lost the row count as she
finished one side and started down another.

Early the next morning
she left behind
her half-started diseño
to tend to the jefes' casas grandes.
As she mopped and dusted and washed all day,
she struggled to keep a pattern in her head
for her eleven P.M. cita—no chaperone allowed—con su hilo y agujas.

We, her sobrinas, have all gone off to the city
to be important people who sit in front of computers.
We've never had the proper time to make our deshilados either,
sea de tela o musica o papel con lapiz.
Instead we spend our time weaving
the intricate fabric of mind-boggling regulations
for the jefes of corporate casas grandes.

On the day years later when the local preacher tried
to honor Tia Maria,
he recalled only her labors for his iglesia bautista:
her years of caring for the white children in the nursery.
He mentioned only that she was a good trabajadora americana.
The entire audience nodded their approval. Even I found myself
somehow proud of Tia Maria's workaholic ways. Maybe because
I remembered
que a las mujeres Palomo / Acosta no se les para ni una mosca.
But I also hung my head in shame that day
for forgetting

Tia Maria's fingers snapping and pulling threads
with a sure speed and a deliberate rhythm.
It is my fault for not standing up and insisting that
her labores included canvases that number in the hundreds.

Only the sound of Tia Maria's sweeping broom would be what
the local paper captured for eternity
in its worn-out vocabulary for writing about
her / us / la chicana hermandad.
But even so, Tia Maria,
although it's too late to tell you in person,
I, your sobrina, must try for forgiveness and homage
con este lapiz en este papel.

2003

I REMEMBER 60.

Fay Yauger

My father rode a horse
And carried a gun;
He swapped for a living
And fought for his fun—
I remember his spurs
A-gleam in the sun.
My father was always
Going somewhere—
To rodeo, market,
Or cattleman's fair—
I remember my mother,
Her hand in the air.

1935

61. MY FATHER AND THE FIGTREE
Naomi Shihab Nye

For other fruits my father was indifferent.
He'd point at the cherry trees and say,
"See those? I wish they were figs."
In the evenings he sat by my bed
weaving folktales like vivid little scarves.
They always involved a figtree.
Even when it didn't fit, he'd stick it in.
Once Joha was walking down the road and he saw a figtree.
Or, he tied his camel to a figtree and went to sleep.
Or, later when they caught and arrested him,
his pockets were full of figs.

At age six I ate a dried fig and shrugged.
"That's not what I'm talking about!" he said,
"I'm talking about a fig straight from the earth—
gift of Allah!—on a branch so heavy it touches the ground.
I'm talking about picking the largest fattest sweetest fig
in the world and putting it in my mouth."
(Here he'd stop and close his eyes.)

Years passed, we lived in many houses, none had figtrees.
We had lima beans, zucchini, parsley, beets.
"Plant one!" my mother said, but my father never did.
He tended garden half-heartedly, forgot to water,
let the okra get too big.
"What a dreamer he is. Look how many things he starts
and doesn't finish."

The last time he moved, I got a phone call.
My father, in Arabic, chanting a song I'd never heard.
"What's that?"
"Wait till you see!"

He took me out to the new yard.
There, in the middle of Dallas, Texas,
a tree with the largest, fattest, sweetest figs in the world.
"It's a figtree song!" he said,
plucking his fruits like ripe tokens,
emblems, assurance
of a world that was always his own.

1989

SURF FISHING   62.
Sarah Cortez

Daddy taught me — warm
Gulf tugging up our chests
and through long pants.

Bait bucket
on a leader
of white rope.

Always too much sand
to see into the water. But
once in a while
a mouth or claws
came for our legs or toes.

Sarah Cortez

Mostly, we pulled up perch.
Less than pan-sized
got thrown back.

White flesh,
rainbowed scales, dark
unwavering eyes.

Mom collected driftwood, built
a fire. Fried our catch in heavy
cast-iron, grease sputtering.

Starbursts of cornmeal,
pepper and salt,
in kerosene lantern light.

We slept leeward
of our car but awoke
with salty grit everywhere. All
for the love of surf rolling in,
white crests against warm blackness,
eerie trickles of wind.

2007

63. THE LITTLE BROTHER POEM
Naomi Shihab Nye

I keep seeing your car in the streets
but it never turns at our corner. I keep finding
little pieces of junk you saved, a packing box, a white rag,
and stashed in the shed for future uses. Today I am cleaning
the house. I take your old camping jug, poke my finger
through the rusted hole in the bottom, stack it on the trash
wondering if you'd yell at me, if you had other plans for it.

Little brother, when you were born I was glad. Believe this.
There is much you never forgave me for but I tell you now,
I wanted you.

It's true there are things I would change. Your face bleeding
the day you followed me and I pushed you in front of a bicycle.
For weeks your eyes hard on me under the bandages. For years
you quoted me back to myself, mean things I'd said that I didn't
remember. Last summer you disappeared into the streets of Dallas
at midnight on foot crying and I realized you'd been serious,
some strange bruise you still carried under the skin.
You're not little anymore. You passed me up and kept reminding me
I'd stopped growing. We're different, always have been,
you're Wall Street and I'm the local fruit market,
you're Pierre Cardin and I'm a used bandanna.
That's fine, I'll take differences over things that match.

If you were here today we wouldn't say this.
You'd be outside cranking up the lawnmower.
I'd be in here answering mail.
You'd pass through the house and say "You're a big help"
and I'd say "Don't mention it" and the door would close.
I think of the rest of our lives. You're on the edge of yours today.
Long-distance I said "Are you happy?" and your voice wasn't sure.
It sounded small, younger, it sounded like the little brother
I don't have anymore, the one who ran miniature trucks up my arms
telling me I was a highway, the one who believed me
when I told him monkeys arrived in the night to kidnap boys
with brown hair. I'm sorry for everything I did that hurt.
It's a large order I know, dumping out a whole drawer at once,
fingering receipts and stubs, trying to put them back
in some kind of shape so you'll be able to find everything later,
when you need it, and you don't have so much time.

1980

64.   GROWING UP NEAR
                    ESCONDIDO CANYON
                      Walter McDonald

With bristles and picks
precise as diamond cutters,
they chip two hundred years a day,
tagging snake bones and buffalo, bowls
and amulets of teeth.

Here in caliche they've found five flints
buried twelve thousand years,
nothing on either side for centuries
as if they killed each other off,
not even small-boned rabbits,

Layer after layer like diamonds
malleted at bad angles and shattered.
Growing up a mile from here,
I raced my brother
over the plains,

hawks on bent wings
gawking at us, dipping and sidling
on summer thermals.
Years before diggers climbed down
these cliffs, we made up lies

at night—murders, something moaning
across the canyon, bodies
buried in shallow graves,
dug up by dogs and eaten.
My brother found the bones.

In moonlight, trying not to shiver,
afraid our father would catch us
sneaking home,
we huddled by a stick fire
cursing, smoking bark cigars.

Midnight, thinking of what we'd found,
we held them up to the moon,
cows' bones or coyotes'
we believed were human,
turning them over and over.

2002

CHAPTER FOUR

OFFICIAL CREATURES, ALONG WITH FURRY AND FEATHERED RUNNERS-UP

A MOCKING-BIRD 65.
Boyce House

My friend, the football coach in San Antonio,
And I were talking about his team, sitting on the little
porch in the edge of town at sundown,
When from a tree across the street there came a song
As though rainbows and silver-edged waves and Persian
fragrances had been woven into throbbing sound.
I knew what it was though never before had I heard the
singer.
But, to make sure, eagerly I asked my friend.
"It's only a mocking-bird,"
And he kept on talking about long punts and forward passes,
And how the quarterback forgot to use Number Forty-seven
last Saturday.

1950

DUET 66.
Betsy Feagan Colquitt

On this April afternoon as Texas heat revs up,
curtains and windows open as the turned-up radio
carries the Met's *La Bohème* into the yard.
As the soprano begins her aria
Si. Mi chiamano Mimi,
ma il mio nome é Lucia.
La storia mia é breve
the only outside sounds are live oak leaves
moving in concert with the slow breeze,
but as her song continues,
another singer listens, likes

Betsy Feagan Colquitt

Mimi's melody, and modestly—
he's no professional—
does a fast warm-up, a little vocalize,
a bit of solfège, and though not a tenor,
turns Mimi's aria into a duet.

He's a quick study, good at timing,
follows her tempo, melodic line
taking it down a 3rd, a 5th, even a 7th
to show his range. Knowing no Italian,
he sings unworded notes,
loves harmonizing—
even tries a bit of vibrato—
and is as smitten as Rodolfo.
He's joyful, amazed at what two singers
can do, at how "music" fills
this quicksilver air
her song and his.

As Mimi sings Sono la sua vicina
Che la vien fuori d'ora a importunare,
and clapping and bravos break the spell,
his interest fails before non-music,
and as mockers do, he goes his way,
no looking, thinking back, no lament
that his addenda to Puccini
is unscored and beyond transcription.

1997

MR. BLOOMER'S BIRDS   67.

William D. Barney

A man needs something animal
to be attached to, thought Mr. Bloomer,
a cur, a nag, a wench. The rumor
of a soul requires a body of fact.
Therefore, nothing is more logical
than that I grant these birds a pact.

And that was how the grackles, boat-tailed,
interior-becandled eye,
took over Belton. Bloomer was why:
he welcomed them with open ears.
The timber-creak in any oaken throat
musicked him more than chanticleers

or nightingales, or even thrushes
(none such in any town he'd dwelt in).
The way those old cocks swaggered spelt in
Bloomer's book, the mark of the elite.
He wasn't one for holy hushes;
he liked a gabble, settling down to eat.

Lord, how he loved those tails! though what
they had to do with boats he never
was able to guess, not being clever.
Nature endowed with plenty to spare—
he watched them waggle in a strut
and he admired more than men dare

on most street corners. Birds can be hatched
in any town, but the boat-tails knew
a platform when they found it. You

might say they hungered for an audience.
True artists need someone attached.
And there was Bloomer in his innocence.

1969

68.

WHOOPING CRANE
James Marion Cody

At the outer edge again
of my universe
in the Canadian North.
At the end of my journey, in Vancouver,
I could turn North again
and leave my past.
But I will go South
not knowing where my soul goes,
and what, or if, it will accomplish.
But South I must go to Texas again
like the reason of no reason
in the head of
a whooping crane.

1993

69.

HAWKS IN A BITTER BLIZZARD
Walter McDonald

Hard work alone can't drive blue northers off.
Nine blizzards out of ten blow out
by Amarillo, nothing this far south

but flakes and a breeze to make a man
in shirt sleeves shiver. Every few years,
Canada roars down, fast-freezing cattle

in the fields, dogs caught between barns,
hawks baffled on fence posts. Stubborn,
hawks refuse to hunker down in burrows

with drowsy rattlesnakes and rabbits.
They drown in their own breath-bubbles,
crystal as the sheen on barbed wires

freezing in the rain. Wood carvers driving by,
grinding on chains down icy roads,
see them at dawn and envy, tempted

to haul the fence posts home and burn them,
nothing in oak or juniper they carve
ever as wild and staring as those eyes.
1989

A RUFOUS-CROWNED SPARROW SEEN LOITERING BELOW POSSUM KINGDOM DAM   70.

William D. Barney

That dry inhabitant of clay,
of postoak copse and sandstone cliff
comes to the fence as though to say
he'd no valid objection if
we kept a distance reasonably trim—
we'd make no difference to him

if we did nothing startlinger
than gawk admiringly at one
with a red pate and black whisker.
No use to think comparison:
he knew himself to be unique
from round of tail to wedge of beak.

Why anyone so fashionably dressed
would live aridly, in seclusion—
the cause is better left unguessed:
rare things come scarcely in profusion,
I told myself, growing profound.
(He cocked his head, the rufous-crowned.)
1969

71. HILL COUNTRY BIRD WOMAN
for Ammie Rose
Jan Epton Seale

Jan Epton Seale

In the comics she was feathered, fierce.
She whooshed down to haul you off.
She had a consort and a cohort.
She sprang from an unholy union
of peacock and pterodactyl.

But our Bird woman is pink,
carries a white downy crown,
walks black-slippered.
This morning she's descended
to open ground, field glasses set.
She declares an oak tree just ahead
to be a clock. If we're lucky,
we'll see her phoebe at ten-thirty.
Bird Woman lowers her glasses.

Now he's the gone-away bird.
Birds are as natural as oatmeal.
They rattle or fuss or tick.
They perch in her dreams in color,
except for egrets, grackles,
and lamb-eating eagles
consigned to black and white.
In nightmares, birds bang at windows,
are gobbled by rat snakes,
flit off without showing
crucial breast or chin or vent.
She wakes weeping,
says the light was poor,
seeks consolation in the arms
of her snowy-crested mate,
a birder-by-marriage.

Our Lady of Hill Country Birds
will talk to a streak of air,
a shaking bush, a jiggling branch.
Birds are holy secrets she incants
in morning vapors or twilights.
For birds' sakes she will humor
the lazy eye, the weak memory,
the best intention.

But Bird Woman has her principles:
"Nature is not always kind."
"Mockingbirds do indeed mock."
"The bluebird is a difficult feeder."
"Sparrows make such good practice."

And her limits:
"You will see more sparrows
than I would wish for you to see."

"God has not granted me the privilege
of loving the boat-tailed grackle."

"Cardinals are worse about getting
into habits than we are."

"Some birders are prone to see
too many exotic birds."

Bird Woman is climbing to aviary nirvana.
If Bird Woman seeks the big Why,
she's nesting it secret as a hummer's egg.
What she likes is the Is of the bird.

So she's chanting its name like a charm,
willing it out of harm's way,
tagging it with love,
declaring a bird is a letter from God
feather-wrapped and sent airmail.

2005

72.   ANNIVERSARY TRIP

James Hoggard

It was not evil, though it looked that way,
the copperhead wrapped around a branch
four feet from our eyes by the Brazos,
a river once called Arms of God

After beaching our canoe for lunch
we had lain on a slope on the bank
then moved to a clearing for shade
where a breeze, sliding coolly now
through our loosened clothes,

fingered its way across us,
a salt cedar brake and scrub oak mott
screening us from public view

Letting skin see in its own oblique way,
I let my gaze drift, but my breath
disappeared, my eyes now locked
on an oddly long knot

twisted on a branch twisted before us,
and the dark ragged bands were not wood,
and the shotlike red eyes did not blink

Look straight ahead, I said, don't move

And fingernails now biting blood
from our palms, we rose,
and the brush seemed to watch us,
as slowly we moved away

in a way we have not always done,
memory saying we'd see that snake
everywhere we looked the rest of the day

2000

James Hoggard

TO THE RATTLESNAKE 73.
Vaida Stewart Montgomery

Old Rattler, we have known each other long—
Both natives of the arid Texas plains—
Where hate is hate, and friendship's ties are strong,
And red blood flows in every creature's veins.
In infancy I lay upon my bed

And did not fear that you would do me harm:
I saw you coiled, I saw your swaying head
And heard your buzzing rattles give alarm.

My father clipped your head off with his gun,
My mother pressed me to her, strangely pale,
He turned your shining belly to the sun
And cut the dozen rattles from your tail.

Old Rattler, it is part of Nature's plan
That I should grind you underneath my heel—
The age-old feud between the snake and man—
As Adam felt in Eden, I should feel.

And yet, Old Rattlesnake, I honor you;
You are a partner of the pioneer;
You claim your own, as you've a right to do—
This was your Eden—I intruded here.

1930

RATTLESNAKE ROUNDUP
74.
Pat Stodghill

(The Sweetwater Jaycees sponsor an annual rattlesnake roundup in Sweetwater, Texas. No firearms are allowed and the snakes must be brought in alive. Gas is used to drive them from their dens.)

I
Seeking fresh air
they crawl out of the den
curving slowly, hibernation stiff...
crooked brown scaly ribbons,
diamond etched,

wrinkling over the rough rocks.
Their spade heads rise,
eyes staring, forked tongues flickering.

II
The hunters wait,
armed with nooses, wire cages, forked sticks.
It is March, but the men sweat,
sweat as the snakes coil…
dung heaps with heads raised, tails rattling.

III
Bringing innate fear, the people come,
armed with legends…
mystic powers of evil, sex, fertility, rain, immortality…
to sit on the hard benches under the lights and girders
in the Nolan County Coliseum,
to stare back at alien eyes,
to watch ten thousand snakes wind around each other in the pit
forming one brown mass of moving…
heads leading, slowly sliding,
curving under and around, tangled together,
winding and unwinding…
even after the lights go out.

1970

ARMADILLO
Martin S. Shockley

75.

Ambling across aeons to my backyard,
she pokes her little snout into my mind,
ancient cousin from my dismal past.
The dinosaurs were gone, the reptiles going,

Martin S. Shockley

when this mammalian experiment was designed:
armored against the menace of the world,
warm-blooded mother, leaving no cold eggs
to hatch in the hot sand,
she severs flesh from flesh
and suckles it, presaging me.

Cornered beneath my juniper, she digs,
and in a moment burrows out of sight.
I grasp her scaly tail and pull;
she holds in tight;
I have to dig her up.
Trailing zoology, she ambles off.

I, tool-using primate, hold with my spade
dominion over armadillos.

1967

COYOTE

76.

Jim Linebarger

Sunday afternoons
my father would idle our '38 Chevy
across the rutted prairie of West Texas,
a fine rifle cradled on his arm.

When we were lucky, we'd see one of them.
He would end up hanging from bobwire,
unravelling in the wind.

Last month, asleep here in my house
in what they call a development,
here where my neighbor's stationwagon
brags that he's a country squire,
I woke to a wild yelping.
The dogs had cornered something.
Next morning, Old Casey showed up
with a neatly-clipped ear
and whined and favored a foreleg.

This morning, I looked out
and saw him shy away
as the coyote calmly trotted
toward the food-scraps in the yard.
Pointed muzzle, scraggy tail, mottled coat.

Camera in hand, I eased the door open.
He bolted. I missed him.

Dad is nearly blind. Casey seems resigned.

I hope you're here to stay.

1989

77.

THE HORSE IN MY YARD
Gene Shuford

In the morning of my manswarmed days
the night breaks open as I come and find
a horse grazing in my yard.
The sun burnishes his winter coat and he throws his head
high in the dawn's burning, aflame on the wick
of night. He has lifted the wire, walked through my fence,
ignoring the barbs. And stands four-footed, firm
as stone, a great shaggy stone horse
planted immovable against the smoking sky.
But then, moving slowly, with immense dignity,
lifting his long muzzle, he stares at me,
at trees green-fired with spring, at passing birds.
How many of us find our fences broken,
our spiked strands ignored, big footprints
inside our barriers? He lets his long
mane whip in the dawn like some wind-flown flag,
rippling in graceful, soundless arpeggios of light;
moves the way thought moves, or dreams, or music;
hunches his big muscles, lowers his head,
and resumes eating. The grass is his business—
my grass—snipped with unbroken rhythm.
You'll say it's Texas—that horses come into yards
in Texas. I'll answer there's no yard where a horse
may not enter, walk big-hooved out of the dark—
no fence where the barbs may not be lifted, strands
thrust apart, snapped if need be.
Of course this is Texas. A land where the heart lives,
sky is infinite, wind blows forever,
and the distance from here to there stretches past
the atom's core. It's more than big hats.
Or six-guns. Or rusted spurs. Or hanging trees.

Or dreams jet-flown from Texarkana west—
clear to El Paso—smell the dust. Or drives
of cattle north to past's remembered green.
Or sun spinning between now and what has been.
Tomorrow's the answer sought and not yet read.
This business of the fence. Heel flies send
a cow across, through, under wire,
ripping it apart as though cobwebbed
by patient spiders—a gangling, lank cow
bawling her glazed bellow, galloping drunk,
leaping beyond the horizon. The horse comes through.
Like a man, he lifts the wire, walks in,
stands now four-footed against the sky.
It all goes back to land, to the time when horses
thundered across unfenced prairie, the heart's land
beyond all fences, where the grass is green,
where all the stallions come, where mares foal
in spring and colts leap above the sun
and there's a long running no wire can stop.

I did not come to this house alone. I came
booted in spirit, jingle-footed to the music of you.
I came inside the oaks, behind the trees,
to the hill's battlements against the endless sky.
I shut the door behind us, but not the door
against the wind. It blows forever in Texas,
whipping the dust of now to the dust of forever,
spiraling between earth and heaven like a bird
that sings the endless music of eternity.
Yet Texas is not a here, or even a now,
but a place where all men ride, the place they come
to face the end of things. How many of us
find it in our hearts—gunned down by time,
sprawled in the past's muck to the tin-pan tunes

from a corner saloon? We lie death-lidded, eyes
staring sightless at heaven. There it is,
stretching endlessly above us, far beyond
the birds. All we have to do is see—

1969

78.   CATTLE
                        Berta Hart Nance

Other states were carved or born,
Texas grew from hide and horn.

Other states are long or wide,
Texas is a shaggy hide,

Dripping blood and crumpled hair;
Some fat giant flung it there,

Laid the head where valleys drain,
Stretched its rump along the plain.

Other soil is full of stones,
Texans plow up cattle-bones.

Herds are buried on the trail,
Underneath the powdered shale;

Herds that stiffened like the snow,
Where the icy northers go.

Other states have built their halls,
Humming tunes along the walls.

Texans watched the mortar stirred,
While they kept the lowing herd.

Stamped on Texan wall and roof
Gleams the sharp and crescent hoof.

High above the hum and stir
Jingle bridle-rein and spur.

Other states were made or born,
Texas grew from hide and horn.

1931

WIND AND HARDSCRABBLE 79.
Walter McDonald

It's wind, not rain, dry cattle need.
Vanes of windmills spinning all day
turn lead pipes into water.
Wind makes metal couplings sough
like lullabies. As long as there is wind,
calm steers keep grazing, believing

there is always water. On still days
steers are nervous,
lashing their tails at horseflies
always out of reach. They stomp
flat hooves and tremble, bleeding,
and thrust their dehorned heads

between barbed wires. When it blows,
steers don't need heaven.

Wind is mystery enough.
They rasp dry tongues across salt blocks,
eyes closed, and wind brings
odors of grainfields miles away.

                Even in drought they feast,
the curled grass crisp as winter stubble.
Parched, they wade still pastures
shimmering in heat waves
and muzzle deep in stock tanks
filled and overflowing.

1985

80. WASHING THE COW'S SKULL
David C. Yates

Most people, I suppose, would rather not wash one,
would not even think of washing one, would leave
it lying there in the pasture, its chalky
white bone baking in the summer Texas sun.

My son Scott found one lying under a mesquite
behind Ed Greenberger's abandoned ranch house.
He cradled it in his arms and I had a recollection:
Ed riding along the edge of his pasture,

his '41 Dodge pickup bouncing over ruts,
Ed eyeballing his cattle, watching them graze
fat on rich Coastal Bermuda, Ed smiling,
his tan face wrinkled, his Stetson tilted forward.

Daddy, let's wash it, wash it clean again!
I look at Scott's deep brown eyes, radiant, alive,

then stare into that skull's deep, empty sockets,
and the sun washes the sky pink as it elbows

its way off the edge of the prairie, and I shudder
at that dirty old hunk of bone with its hollow earpassages
and yellowing jaws laced with yellow teeth
set loosely in bony yellow gums so they

click like dice when Scott runs his fingers
along their moldy crowns. This skull once had
a tongue in it, and it could moo once, Scott said,
and I knew, then, that washing the skull

was what we were going to do. Scott held it
in his lap as we drove towards West Beach,
and we stopped at a U-Tote-M for a scrub brush, a can
of Ajax, some paper towels and two tooth brushes.

That night, while the waves lapped against our legs
and the moon reflected on the water, we washed
that cow's skull till it was as white as a gull's
belly, and it seemed to smile as we brushed its teeth.

1982

❦

CHAPTER FIVE

WEATHER?

WELL IT CAN BE FRIGID
IN FRIONA WHILE
BLISTERING
IN LA BLANCA.
WITH THAT GIVEN,
THE GENERAL CLIMATE IS
HOT

NOVEMBER 81.

James Hoggard
for John Graves

Shimmering spreads of golden fire,
oak leaves fan Comanche Bluff
where the Brazos de Dios turns deep
against a cliff, high limestone wall,
current speeding up at the curve
hard toward a white water roar:
shouts of giants trapped in rock,

and a russet granite boulder,
monolithic in the river's wide rush,
organizes the water slapping at it:
whirlpools drilling into sinkholes,
and down them cold November purls
when fierce blue northern winds
come beating the brilliance off limbs.
1991

A MYTHOLOGY OF SNOW 82.

Violette Newton

Here in the warm counties
in cold months, we practice
a mythology of snow. Long before
Texas plays A&M and fall coats
and boots are everywhere, shop windows
quiver in icicles, and gawky girl
models step like giraffes through
glittered cotton on their way
to a winter never coming.

As leaves fall and grass burns brown
from frost, the myth builds. We spray
foam on cross-batted windows, and
snowmen in mufflers come out
of closets to stand around,
pretending carols.
But when snow really comes,
we never know what to do with it.
Our heating systems quit, our tires
won't grip, our vegetation falls
in a heap. But we go on kidding
ourselves that this is the season
of snow, and as long as we
believe it, we can run around
in our sunclothes, shivering
ourselves into Currier and Ives
impossibilities, knowing
in the hard core of our minds,
no matter what scientists and
weathermen say, snow is pure
imagination anyway, it doesn't
last, it is only icing on the plain
cake of winter, which, in our case,
is only make-believe most of the time.

It takes more than snow, imitation
or otherwise, to make Christmas,
which can happen anywhere, even
in the warm rooms of the heart.

1981

JANUARY LULL (HOUSTON, TEXAS)   83.
Larry D. Thomas

Yet another morning
the sky is pewter
in this wet,
January lull

between freezes.
The only sun
we'll see for days
is terra cotta

saturate with rain,
hanging from a plank
of weathered cedar
in the patio.

Cupped hands
jut from its chin,
offering their chartreuse
gift of moss.

2007

ENNUI   84.
Lawrence Chittenden

At a lonely ranch 'neath a lonely sky
On the tawny Texas prairie,
Where the owls hoo, and the plovers cry,
And the cayotes howl, and the Northers sigh,
To-night I am sad and weary.

The fire dreams on in its chimney-bed,
While the rain on the roof is sobbing
A requiem sad for a year that's dead,
For the shadowy faces flown and fled,
For the days misspent, and the words unsaid,
And the dreams that Time is robbing.

Without, in the wind and rain and gloom,
The night is steeped in sorrow,
While spectral fancies haunt my room
With ghostly thoughts from Memory's tomb,
And the cares of a dull To-morrow.
Ah, Life is at best a lonely lane
O'ergrown with the rue and roses,
Though the flowers must wither, the thorns remain,
For each heart knoweth some secret pain;
Some fond regret, and some hope in vain,
In each secret reposes.

Hast thou not sighed for some ideal shore
'Midst groves and forests vernal—
Where pain and trials and griefs were o'er,
Where the world was fair as dreams of yore,
Where hearts were true and life was more,
And love was a thing Eternal?
Ah, yes! and to-night 'neath a lonely sky,
On the tawny Texas prairie,
Where the owls hoo and the Northers sigh,
Where the cayotes wail, and the plovers cry,
To-night I am sad and weary.
December 31st

1893

WINTER IN TEXAS
William V. Davis

85.

It is grey today, but there is no snow.
Snow is rare here—once or twice a year,
one year in ten. Even so, it gets cold,
and it is cold today. Indeed, it is the kind of day in which one
might expect snow
in places where snow can be expected.
I have lived in such places and I miss them
The way I miss the snow. I now know
That it will only be after I have died,
Only then—when my body has been buried
Near where I first learned to love snow —
Will I again feel the snow, falling thick
and light, and deep and slow, through air
and trees on days like these.

2003

EARLY WARNING
Frederick Turner

86.

Spring comes in Dallas like a gunshot, like
A big transformer fuse, a missile strike.
Ninety degrees. Over the northern grid
Dances a disembodied pyramid.
Foam and dark water dries up in a flash
On the white-hot forecourt of the car-wash.
Air has the lilac tremor of cocaine,
Matter's dissolved to flakes of cellophane.
All along Hillcrest and Arapaho
Rises, pinkwhite, a radioactive glow
Of blanched pearblossom, apple, plum and quince,

Black redbud cankered with flushed innocence.
Don't drive there with the window open; you'll
Fall sick with the flower fumes. It's april fool,
It's mayday, mayday. Photochemical,
The carolina jasmine's cadmium fireball
Batters the sidewalk with a yellow shock
Releasing a sweet gas of poppycock.
The crocuses poke up their noses. "Urk!"
They gasp, and open with a purple jerk.
Don't know if that's blue sky or a fresh storm
The sun shines into, giddy, white and warm.
Yes, it's a cloud. The weathermap has grown
A newborn thunderworld all of its own,
Mushrooming up, neon and shadowhazy.
Out of it hail will tumble soon like crazy.
It smells of black disk brake powder, of guns,
Of pyramids and glass and pentagons.
Better take shelter in an underpass.
City of all desires, city of glass.

2000

87. SPRINGTIME IN TEXAS
Walter McDonald

Armadillos drop like dollops
along back highways to Dallas.
They die a mile apart, some belly up,
some like bronzes in Neiman Marcus.

Racing by thickets of mesquite
and live oaks sucked by mistletoe,
I slow to sixty to watch bluebonnets
and Indian blankets dazzle the roadside.

Pickups and cars zip past, a blur of tires
and bumpers daring porcupines
to waddle across, just try it.
We need a chicken to cross the road

to prove to armadillos and skunks
that it could be one. Flat pelts
are closer than a mile apart,
pounded by truckers, meat enough

for crows and buzzards rising
as I approach, polite as diners
in crowded cafes in Guthrie,
Seymour, any West Texas town.

2003

SPRING IN EAST TEXAS   88.
Edward H. Garcia

In spring turtles waken
Not spring to life exactly
Stretch rather, try one clawed leg at a time
Peel an eye for sunrays
To warm cold blood
Lumber up, suddenly hungry
Still slow to rouse
Not riotous like marigolds or periwinkles
Not velvet to the touch like the regal, lovely iris
Slow and rough, slow and rough,
Yet spring.

Edward H. Garcia

I fear I am no longer a flower
Given to riotous rebirth.
Spring comes for me slow and rough,
Slow and rough, yet spring.

2007

89.

SUMMER BEGINS OUTSIDE DALHART, TEXAS

Mary Vanek

Clouds chinked together vertebrae fashion,
sunspots gilding the last of the winter wheat
make this May day the first true burst of summer.
School's out, littering the yard with children
tumbling over combines pulled out for repairs.
Mothers mutter "lockjaw" and wade in,
scattering kids, denying them the forbidden
sweet of rust in first blood ripped free
on a wingnut ragged with wear and winter rain.
Tonight, the aloe vera plants will be torn
and squeezed to relieve the first sunburns
of the season. And in their cool beds,
the children dream of dinosaur angels
in the sky, those bumpy, lumpy clouds
clear evidence of their belief
in a past alive and pressing as the present.

1989

SUMMER NIGHTS IN TEXAS 90.
Grace Noll Crowell

Days must be hot to make the cotton white,
And have their own peculiar yellow glare,
But when the Gulf wind booms its way at night,
There is no lovelier darkness anywhere.
I lift my face—I turn toward the South,
My hair blows loose—the wind along my path
Is like a drink to any thirsty mouth;
Is like a plunge in some soft-water bath.
I drink the wind! I bathe in it! I dive,
With outstretched arms, a swimmer in my glee!
The wind has made me gloriously alive,
Its waves roll in, and they sweep over me!
No day can be too hot, too long and bright,
If it be followed by a Texas night.

1936

91.

SUMMER NIGHTS
Paul Christensen

Where the tracks sidewind through
tall grass, among the tumbledown shacks
of the Brazos bottoms, the boys
stand around keeping the moon company,
bottle in hand, swapping tall tales
and curses until the girls go dancing.

And the stark white houses rot in silence
with their lonely beds, and the heat
thick in the parlors, the old men
sleeping in their Lazy Boy loungers

before the muttering tv, the farm wives
playing bingo in the gymnasium

while the lights hum in the dance hall
and the smell of sugar and sweat
mix in the breath, as an arm
goes tense with the feel of skin
in its bony hand, and a softness
wild as the sea gives in to love.

1994

Alan Birkelbach

92. EVENT, CLARITY
Alan Birkelbach

In Lubbock, in the middle of summer nights,
when the power would go out and the fans would die on us,
then we would remember the cast iron bed
had wheels, so we would creakily negotiate it

out the door and across the yard
and park it there in clear view of the road, and you'd wear something flannel
and I'd wear faded boxers,

and you'd lay your head on my chest.
The moon was an icebox cooling our eyes and cheeks;
it was white and pocked like a thin,
late Winter Texas snow,

and we would watch satellites
drift overhead like determined fireflies,
watch them blink steady like breaths we had to take,
like our heartbeats measuring the length of night.

2007

RIDING THE CURRENTS 93.
Susan Bright

I want to ride the currents,
find light in the shallows
of the emerald water,
cool under an August sun
that heats Texas to a sizzle.

I want to ride the currents,
move my legs back and forth,
kick exactly these red flippers
that push me through
the water, four long laps
in cold emerald light—
an elegant, rich mile.
I want to sit alongside
Barton Springs and talk
to my friends, the swimmers
who have been meeting here
for years, new swimmers,
water people whose eyes are
clear as emerald, and true.

I want to ride the currents,
draft the swimming god,
smooth the jagged edges
of me that shred any hope

Susan Bright

127

of serenity. I want to disappear
into the water, no seams.

I want to ride the currents,
not always fight them,
kick back and stretch,
swim further today
than I could yesterday,
and faster because it makes
me strong, because
it calms me down.

2001

94.   HAIKU: LAZY AFTERNOON
Michael A. Moore

Lazy Afternoon
Floating in a summer dream
Guadalupe day.

2007

95.   DROUGHT: SURE SIGNS IN MERKLE, TEXAS
Robert A. Fink

The Farmers' Life insurance agent
washed his company car three times this week,
parked it in the driveway overnight.
Come Monday and no thunder,
he'll wax the pickup.

My next door neighbor forgets to close
his back porch windows when he leaves for work
and the retired couple up the street
started yesterday to paint their house.
They claim they're bored with last summer's color.

Ten miles west of here, Jimmie Ruth's father
shot a rattlesnake and hung it from
the top strand of his barbed wire fence.
He noticed small birds walking backwards.
An owl flew over the house at noon.

But I.M. Richards and Mr. Petre
down at Miller's Feed & Seed farmed here in '52.
I.M. shuffles the dominoes
and spits into a box of sand,
swears this ain't nothing:
"The sky's still blue.
Nobody's seen a buzzard in the street.
And Truman's rheumatiz is acting up.
Pull yourself a chair and play this round.
We'll tell you when it's time to call the preacher."

1989

SAN ANTONIO MI SANGRE: FROM THE HARD SEASON 96.
Naomi Shihab Nye

We have faith that God… is the owner of water and the
one who could really help us with this.
Rev. Rodolfo Ruiz, during prayers for the drought

Naomi Shibab Nye

The 2 A.M. whistle of the long train
stretches out the thread between days,

pins it in a crack between its teeth and pulls
so the people in white beds by the flour mill

become the wheat
underground in the sacks

and the old fish with one whisker
slips over in the river grown too thin.

We need the rain, the iron bar of the track,
the backside of heat. Perfect V-ripple eleven ducklings
cast swimming toward the shore for bread.

As the boys who will not lift their heads
to look anyone in the eye mark the name of their pack

on the bridge with the stink of squared-off letters,
Señora Esquivel who lives alone

remembers her underwear draped on the line.
It will not rain tonight, has not rained in 90 nights.

Cantaloupe cracks on the inside,
jagged fissures in orange flesh.

When the cat blinks to see the sneaky possum
licking his water dish dry,

he thinks, and thinks. Tomorrow I'll get him.
Then sleeps. Inside the small breeze

lifting the fringe of the train's held tone
Hondo, Sabinal, Uvalde, Del Rio, and far off,

glittering as Oz, El Paso rising
from its corner, holding the giant state in place

as a dozing conductor grips his swatch of tickets firmly
in a car streaking the thirsty land.

1998

AFTER THE RANDOM TORNADO   97.
Walter McDonald

Harvest won't save our barn from twisters
on plains as flat as the moon. A keg of nails
can't make old rafters safe for owls
and heifers mild as saints. The last tornado

smashed the church a mile away like match sticks,
sinners saved by grace. Lucky for cows,
the twister froze, veered off
and left their calves alone. Our barn's a maze

of tin and splinters, nothing to do but tear it down
and raise one better for bumper crops.
Fat cattle are in our fields, all fences tight,
a pasture of calves all spring.

But watch the stingy cirrus clouds for signs—
buzzards circling the gate, angels prowling
in the shape of funnels, beggars needing to be fed.
Pray that our gates bring strangers.

Give away grain overflowing the silos,
press beggars in from the road and clothe them,
send riders to warn our cousins
beware of angels seeking work.

2000

98. MR. WATTS AND THE WHIRLWIND
William D. Barney
(Andre Watts Recital, TCU)

William D. Barney

On Cantey Street a visitor came by
doing a dervish dance in the parking lot.
But we didn't know. We were listening
to Mr. Watts play the *Appassionata*.
(I almost thought it was old Ludwig
softly applauding, but it was thunder,
faint as the sirens, off-stage.)
Beethoven would have approved, though.
The hands that delicately touched
Scarlatti now smote the stays
and timbers of the Steinway
until it moaned with joy.

We had known, of course, there was danger.
Before Mr. Watts came from the wings
a third time, a messenger appeared:
"A tornado has touched down not far—
it must be determined whether
we ought to proceed to the basement."
But we were safe; and Mr. Watts began.
At intermission we learned more—
The twister really had come by, and we

all left to see the destruction.
Autos on top one another or shoved aside
as by an impatient hand, canty
off Cantey Street, you might say,
if only a few. It was all random.
Not at all like that perfect storm
Mr. Watts cleanly and powerfully
struck on the keys and strings.
Maybe it heard and was jealous. It was
a fairly minor tornado as winds go.
But we who had ears will remember
how the two touched down all at once,
a finger of terror from the skies,
those hands of unthinkable skill.

1999

ABILENE, TX: WE PULL OUT FOR NEW ENGLAND 99.

Robert A. Fink

There is a reason why the compass needle
time and again lays its seam due north.
If you believe an icy lodestone peaks atop the globe
then you'll buy desert property in Arizona.
The truth is it points home,
the place we started from so long ago
we've lost the recollection of our skin as smooth,
blood thick enough to flow through winter.

Now we are turning back from this land of sky,
the punctual sun wide as all horizons.
Back from the saucy mockingbird

who owns us all. The shy snake of diamonds
coiling his warning. Back down
the oil smooth highway spilled across forever.
The neighbors seem to understand
shaking their heads at what they know
may one day come for them.

The mesquites are sad. Their leaves point us out
for shame. We could endure. Grow tough
sinking tap roots deep, tributaries wide.
We, too, could learn the signs of spring,
how to judge when winter's really passed.
We, too, could learn to camel out the summer.
I want to shout from the station wagon window:
WE'RE COMING BACK. IT'S JUST FOR JUNE TO AUGUST.
The trees know better. Another squatter gone,
run out of town by bullies.
IT'S NOT LIKE THAT! Surprised
I roll the window up, refuse to speak for miles.

1984

100.   110 DEGREES IN DALLAS   SEP 4
Frederick Turner

A few vague clouds in the insane blue sky.
The rabbits on the grass are stunned and tame.
A milk-green mantle chokes the shrunken stream.
A hackberry, heat-shocked, begins to die.
The summer suburbs give off one long hum
Of worn compressors fading with a sigh.
A parched cicada shrieks and then falls dumb.

The grackles march, beak gaped, with deranged eye.
The summer's now so old it's lost its mind.
It's quite forgotten what's the way to rain.
The sun sees everything, except it's blind.
The sky, as we begin, is still insane.
This is the test of all that life can stand.
And being, being presses on the land.

2000

GOOD-BYE SUMMER 101.
Jas. Mardis

With the blaring Texas sun beating down against my bent back
I am waving good-bye to Summer with my spine

I am waving good-bye
by arching that spindled thread of bone
    and warm, pulsing blood
    as the last offering to this Pompeii of a season

Jas. Mardis

Bending it
    gracing the face of this heat monger
    gracing the face of this too long visitor
this too long stayed relative
    from both sides of the family
  whom no one can remember
having invited

I am waving good-bye to Summer with my bent back
        my curved spine
      my chaffed and scarlet, naked bottom
to avoid her seeing my face

I am hiding
    bent and red with the heat of this Summer sun on my back
and I am pounding my fist into the parched earth
     calling out the damnation
  carving out the dry land with my fingers
as my proof
that it is time for the sun to go

and there is a chorus of brown flowers
with their stems long turned to wilting
and there are young summer grasses
   never known to our eyes as green
and there are panting dogs
with tongues dragging the pavement
and there are drying water holes
with the catfish and bass
     flipping on their sides
          gasping for air, then water, then air

And I am here to say good-bye to Summer
    and to tell her that I will have no more of it

That I am sick and swollen red enough with her beaming
     sick of her constant blushing
   that draws some under its spell
     and drives them madly into stripping their bodies free of
clothes
and lying for hours under her gaze and torment
   until their skin
  is baked into the red-brown singe
of madness

I am here to say good-bye to Summer
    and to save the singed ones from her torment
    I am here to rid the land of her callous stare

that leans the grasses into kindling for fire
in these months when the rain hides itself in the Midwest
    and like some frightened school boy
wets the land like his pants

    And so I say, Good-bye Summer
Kiss My Backside
   and let this Texas town
know again: a cool gust of wind in the noon hour
or   the late-night whine of chilled breezes through barely
open windows
or   the damp footprints in the sand after a morning rain

Move on Summer
    and make way for the cool days and nights of the next season
  with its bland days of blue skies and gray clouds
  and birds heading North

Make way Summer
   for the damp brow, late season, last picnics of the lovers
who found themselves while cowering from your wrath
  and those children
    who hunger to know their last days of freedom
  with school already started

  I am here to say goodbye to Summer
and her tattered blanket of heat and heat and heat
all the day and night long

  I am here to say a shallow-voiced "Good-bye"
because I know that soon
  I will be calling her back
when the rain and wind have me gripped by the neck
  and there is snow
or just the biting winter wind blowing through my clothes

or
   my toes have turned blue
with my fingers
   frigid and flirting with frostbite
      I will be among the first to scream her sacred name
but until then
I am saying good-bye to this Texas summer
      with my face hidden
and my back turned
   hoping that she doesn't recognize my voice

1993

LONE STAR PEOPLE AND THEIR LAND

THE LITTLE TOWNS OF TEXAS   102
Clyde Walton Hill

The little towns of Texas
That nestle on her plains
And gather close the inland roads,
The homing trails and lanes;
The little towns of Texas
That sleep the whole night long
Cooled by a scented southern breeze,
Lulled by its drowsy song!

The little towns of Texas
Will ever seem to me
Like stars that deck a prairie sky
Or isles that dot the sea:
Like beads that sparkle here and there
On Texas' flowered gown;
Like figures on its rich brocade
Of purple, green and brown.

The little towns of Texas
Seen through the prairie haze,
How fair and fresh and free they lie
Beneath the golden days!
Not crowded in deep valleys,
Not buried in tall trees,
But open to the sun, the rain,
The starlight, and the breeze!

The little towns of Texas,
What pretty names they bear!
There's Echo, Garland, Crystal Springs,
Arcadia, Dawn, and Dare;

There's Ingleside, and Prairie Home,
And Bells, and Rising Star.
God keep them childlike, restful, clean,
Pure as the prairies are!

1924

103. THE ENDURANCE OF POTH, TEXAS
Naomi Shihab Nye

It's hard to know how well a town is when you only swing
through it on suspended Sunday evenings maybe twice a year.
Deserted streets. The dusty faces of stores: elderly aunts with
clamped mouths. I like to think Monday morning still buzzes
and whirls—rounded black autos roll in from farms, women
measure yard goods, boys haul empty bottles to the grocery,
jingling their coins. Nothing dries up. I want towns like Poth
and Panna Maria and Skidmore to continue forever in the flush,
red-cheeked, in love with all the small comings and goings of
cotton trucks, haylifts, peaches, squash, the cheerleader's
sleek ankles, the young farmer's nicked ear. Because if they
don't, what about us in the cities, those gray silhouettes off on
the horizon? We're doomed.

1991

104. SOUTH RIM: BIG BEND NATIONAL PARK
Arthur M. Sampley

From this sheer wall the Indians watched the plain
And saw, as I, the Rio Grande bend
Southward to Mexico, and saw it end
In mountain ridges, fathomless terrain,

Then reappear and slash two thousand feet
Across a mountain's face and carve a land
In wounded rocks and bleeding veins of sand
Until it ceased where sky and mountains meet.

Far as the bending river sweeps they saw
The leagues of stricken ranges north and south,
And they exulted in that zone of drouth
That lay about their mountain like a law,
Nor dreamed that far beyond that river's mouth
Came ruin from which no desert could withdraw.

1948

BIG BEND: LION WARNING   105.
Jan Epton Seale
(a found poem)

A lion has been frequenting this area
It could be aggressive toward humans

If you see a lion
Pick up small children
Stand together
Appear large
Wave hands and shout
Throw stones or sticks
Report sighting to ranger
Do not
Show fear
Crouch down
Run away

2000

106.

DAWN IN EL PASO
Carol Coffee Reposa

Above the cinderblocks
Pocked sidewalks
Beer and Pepsi cans
Lined up along the streets
Like soldiers
Light slides down
The Franklins
In a ragged progress
Drops sun
In charcoal pockets

Purple clefts
Colors shifting
On the mountain face
Like crumpled taffeta
As early morning

Ripples down the rocks
Peels night
From patient stones
In acts
Of random grace.

1998

107.

LEAVING EL PASO
Marian Haddad

I pull out of Chuy's
out of Van Horn
east on I-10

I look behind
me as I take
the turn
wave good-bye
to my mountains
— an hour and a half
away from home

—purple Franklins,
not quite purple
yet—as I know
that you can get
waiting for our sun
to color
this familiar sky

Marian Haddad

2007

PALO DURO CANYON 108.

Larry D. Thomas

A straight
razor,
this wind
of winter

scraping
high plains
till they bleed,
scraping

toward a canyon
where cedar clings
to sheer faces
of cliffs,

clawing roots
into hard
red scabs
of earth,

this wind
of winter
scraping its way
to a canyon rim

where hawks,
slingshot-flung,
scream in dazzling
Texas sun.

2007

109.   MAKES THEM WILD
Susan Bright

When I grew up there were 4 elements, seed stayed where you planted it, earth was deep, black, moist and stayed down—where it belongs. In West Texas, on the Caprock, earth, air, fire and water blow around together in vast confounding walls of wind. It howls through window glass and comes up through cracks in the floor. Wind, it gets so dark sometimes the chickens go to roost. Wind, the old people say it has a nasty breath, they say you know you been in a wind if there's no paint left on your car, if you got sand between your teeth, under your tongue and on the backs of your eyeballs, if you want to inhale water, or stay in bed all day with a papersack over your head. Wind, it blows through your ears and makes you crazy. You'd swear you're on another planet. At night the stars come down so close the Milky Way sloughs layers of solar dust on children sleeping, makes them wild. You wonder how the farmers know whose land will bear their seed. Women, men, children and even pets move slant to the ground. Sparkling eyes and jokes blare out from the dust like miracles, nothing is like it seems. There is one town called Earth. The rest is alien. Space ships land there often. Almost everyone has seen one, they say the Caprock is a magnet. In the middle of Earth is a sign that says: SHOP EARTH. One man from Pampa rents the wind from his cousin and sells power to the electric company. People say he's so crazy that he might be brilliant. They say his cousin is no fool either.

1983

HEAVE ME A MOUNTAIN, LORD! 110.
Jack E. Murphy
(Prayer from the Plainview Rest Home)

Heave me a mountain, Lord,
from this plain land;
heave me a mountain frosted
white, for these scarred eyes
to climb.

Let it rise west, in view
of room 102; I'll give my potted plant
away and sit all day and night
before my window.

Jack E. Murphy

At night when the moon lights
waterfalls, and aspen leaves
reflect its glow I'll have no need
of sleep, I know.

Lord, heave me a mountain
just like the one I knew.…
no timid mountain, Lord, but bold,
with granite temples etched
in canyon walls, reminding me
of You.

When you heave me a mountain, Lord,
there'll be no need to bury me
300 miles away.

Remember, Lord … west of Room 102,
heave my mountain.

1982

111.   COUNTY FAIR
Fay Yauger

I got me dressed for going down
To Teague, the County Seat,
With half my savings on my back,
And half upon my feet.

My father said, "Be careful, son."
My mother said, "Be good."
My sister said, "Bring me a ring
The way a brother should."

The leaves were in the ditches
And haze was on the ridge
The morning I stepped through our fence
And crossed the trestle bridge.

Oh, chimney-pots were smoking.
And flags were in the air
When I came heeling into Teague
To see the County Fair.

I stopped a peddler-woman
And bought a box of corn
That had a small tin bird inside
For blowing like a horn.

I guessed at pebbles in a jar
And had my fortune told
And learned that I would meet a girl
That day, and find her cold.

The cards were right, for very soon
I crowded through a swirl
Of people near a platform
To watch a dancing girl.

And sure I lost my senses
Right there upon the street
From seeing how she tossed her hair
And shook her little feet.

And "Never will I take a wife
To share my roof and bed
Or spend my gold, unless it be
This dancing girl," I said.

But she—She looked me thru and thru
When I had caught her glance
And said, "I think the hicks have come
To clutter up our dance."

And then—"Get on, my fellow,
And see the cattle shows,"
She said, and snapped her finger-tips
Just underneath my nose.

I got me from her curling mouth,
And from her scornful eyes,
And never stopped to ask if I
Had won the guessing prize.

I cut the miles to home by half,
Straight up a mountain side,
And "Hope to God I never see
That girl again," I lied.

My father let me in at dusk,
My mother looked distraught,
My sister lay all night and wept
The ring I had not bought.

My father questioned me of mares,
My mother spoke of lace,
But I had not a word for them—
I'd only seen a face.

They tell me now I am no good
For sending to a fair,
And do not know that only part
Of me came back from there.

They do not know my hands are here
And here my heavy feet,
But that my heart is miles away—
In Teague, the County Seat.

1935

MESQUITE

Robert A. Fink

(A mesquite tree is like an iceberg.
Those roots go a long, long way down.)

A.F. Henderson
West Texas Rancher

Each one the shape of its soul—
knotted like an old squaw
or pliant as young girls naked by a stream.
Tejas Indians, politely accepting the Catholic
word of God, already knew the word for tree of life:
Shade Whose Tap Root Drinks The Desert.
Female. Fat with many children.

For horseless tribes, mesquite beans
served more ways than buffalo.
A good woman ground forty kilograms
of flour a day. Each July, she and her sisters
gathered the beans in baskets woven tight
as that which rescued Moses.
Even during drought years, bean pods fell like manna,
husks curled like Manitou's smile.
The word for bean was the same as that for rain.

Dissolved, mesquite beans cured sore throats;
swallowed, they purged the system.
Medicine men, spitting on their palms,
worked the flour into a paste
some say healed the blind.
Pressed against the cheek and pricked with cactus needles,
the leaves left a blue tattoo—Thumbprint of God—
protection from all evils.

Around 1850, the mesquite spread to grasslands:
Cowboys and trail herds. Soldiers.
Their horses ate the beans,
germinated the seeds and passed them on—
war and cattle trails remembered with mesquite.

Today, ranchers call them Scrub To Burn.
Tares In Wheat. In town,
home owners wear down chainsaws against the trunks
and, being long accustomed to sprinkler systems and
store-bought bread, curse the beans
nothing seems to stop from falling.

1987

113. DEATH RODE A PINTO PONY
Whitney Montgomery

Death rode a pinto pony
Along the Rio Grande,
Beside the trail his shadow
Was riding on the sand.

The look upon his youthful face
Was sinister and dark,
And the pistol in his scabbard
Had never missed its mark.

The moonlight on the river
Was bright as molten ore,
The ripples broke in whispers
Along the sandy shore.

The breath of prairie flowers
Had made the night-wind sweet,
And a mocking bird made merry
In a lacy-leafed mesquite.

Death looked toward the river,
He looked toward the land,
He took his broad sombrero off
And held it in his hand,

And Death felt something touch him
He could not understand.

The lights at Madden's ranch-house
Were brighter than the moon,
The girls came tripping in like deer,
The fiddles were in tune,

And Death saw through the window
That man he came to kill,
And he that did not hesitate
Sat hesitating still.

A cloud came over the moon,
The moon came out and smiled,
A coyote howled upon the hill,
The mocking bird went wild.

Death drew his hand across his brow,
As if to move a stain,
Then slowly turned his pinto horse
And rode away again.

1934

114.

VISITING
Sarah Cortez

Sharp rock jumped
at our car's belly,
driving unpaved streets
to Laredo relatives. The
language I didn't speak—
older girl cousins trilling
Spanish, dressing
for skinny, black-haired boys
in blue suits
while I
sat with the adults
at formica tables,
listening.

2007

115.

AUGUST ON PADRE ISLAND
Walter McDonald

This is no season for old men,
yet here we sit
under beach umbrellas
as if shade could save us.

This sun strips the breath
down to the bone.
Gull feathers fall,
white sails in the Gulf

die for a breeze. Splashing
as waves crash over them,
children puff like balloons
and dive. Cool currents

slide over them like eels.
They burst straight up,
squealing, leaping in a season
that never lasts.

1988

AUSTIN
Karle Wilson Baker

116.

She leans upon her violet hills at ease
At the plains' edge: innocent and secure,
Keeper of sacred fountains, quaintly sure,
Greek draperies fluttering in the prairie-breeze.
She stands tiptoe and looks across the seas,
Where older lands and richer shrines allure,
Wistful, that she is young and crude and poor—
But secret-sure that she is proud as these.

Her sons bring delicate plunder home, to grace
Houses discreet, and gardens sweetly walled—
She is enamored of the fit and fair.
Far-gathered treasures in her love find place:
White peacocks where the prairie-schooners crawled—
Italian roses in her sunburnt hair.

1929

117.

IN AUSTIN REIGNS A
BALD-HEADED QUEEN
Pat LittleDog

Pat LittleDog

when the door opened
a bald-headed woman came into the room
she was taller than everyone
in her white baggy pants
and her head gleamed
with a rubbed spitshine

women stood around her when she stood up
and when she sat down
they all sat as close as they could

they touched her hems and sleeves
they ran their fingers on her shirttails

they laughed when she laughed
and swayed toward her like flowers
on weak stems

oh bald-headed woman
I whispered from my own place at the crowd's
edge
when I go home tonight
I will look for you in my mirror

since then
I have seen only glimpses of her
several times

1982

THE OLD OAK SPEAKS 118.
Margaret Belle Houston

"For five hundred years, Treaty Oak, said to be the widest spreading tree in North America, has stood near the banks of the Colorado River in Austin. It has played a romantic part in the lives of the Indians and in the history of Texas. Beneath it Stephen Austin signed the compact that fixed the boundary line between the land of the Red Men and the town of Austin. The historic tree may soon be destroyed."—*The Poets' Scroll*, 1926

My roots are buried deep in Texas ground.
I grip the harder when the great winds blow.
I lift my face to drink the Texas rain.
I bow beneath her gifts of gentle snow.

I know the near white faces of her stars.
The prairie moon has bathed me centuries long.
From out my heart a million mocking birds
Have flown to fill the prairie world with song.

Comanche, Tejas, in my shadow stand
To pray the great All Father, and to sign
The treaty with young Austin, vowing peace.
Leaving me guardian of the boundary line.

For I am Texas' oldest pioneer,
Have weathered all her changes to this hour.
Have watched her travail and her victory,
Her urgent growth from poverty to power.

She built a city round about my tent
Whose growing towers, how shining fair they seem!
I brood unchanged, yet in my heart I keep
Memory on memory, dream on dream.

And have I known the last sweet Texas Spring?
No more the green beneath, the blue above?
Oh children, for whose hour I watched in hope,
Let me cling longer to the soil I love!

1926

119.

DANGEREUX AVRIL
Teresa Palomo Acosta

Tonight
In my neighborhood HEB where español is le langue
De muchos de nosotros consumidores
I review my French lessons,
Making up a little something—
Dangereux avril—
to entertain myself as I look for cheap food to buy
With my tiny paycheck.

At the bread bin, I consider the bagels
But mainly I talk myself
About where I am heading en los abriles
Que vienen aunque no se con cual dinero.

Dangereux avril.
I repeat it
As I peer into the bread bins
For bagels:
Four on sale for $1.19. I settle on two.
Yes, avril is coming
And in February I am
Already preparing for it:

Sewing spring prints into dresses
And donning them in late winter
To urge on avril's arrival.
To keep appointments with myself.

My corazon turns somersaults
Over decisions I have already made
To walk into el abril donde quiero caminar.
Head out one door.
Into another.
Go from one road
To the next
Au naturel.

In my neighborhood HEB at night
When I wander entre nous, gente cosmica,
I am finding the syllables of my dangereux avril: one at a time.

In the intricately woven strands
Of the raza that surrounds me.
In their knotty threads:
Le dangereux avril
Awaits me.

1992

GOING FOR PEACHES, FREDERICKSBURG, TEXAS
Naomi Shihab Nye

120.

Those with experience look for a special kind.
Red Globe, the skin slips off like a fine silk camisole.
Boy breaks one open with his hands. Yes, it's good,
my old relatives say, but we'll look around.

They want me to stop at every peach stand
between Stonewall and Fredericksburg,
leave the air conditioner running,
jump out and ask the price.

Coming up here they talked about
the best ways to die. One favors a plane crash,
but not over a city. One wants to make sure
her grass is watered when she goes.
Ladies, ladies! This peach is fine,
it blushes on both sides.
But they want to keep driving.

In Fredericksburg the houses are stone,
they remind me of wristwatches, glass polished,
years ticking by in each wall.
I don't like stone, says one. What if it fell?
I don't like Fredericksburg, says the other.
Too many Germans driving too slow.
She herself is German as Stuttgart.
The day presses forward wearing complaints,
charms on its bony wrist.

Actually ladies, (I can't resist),
I don't think you wanted peaches after all,
you just wanted a nip of scenery,
some hills to tuck behind your heads.
The buying starts immediately, from a scarfed woman
who says she gave up teachin' for peachin'.
She has us sign a guest book.
One aunt insists on reloading into her box
to see the fruit on the bottom.
One rejects any slight bruise.
But Ma'am, the seller insists, nature isn't perfect.
Her hands are spotted, like a peach.

On the road, cars weave loose patterns between lanes.
We will float in flowery peach-smell
back to our separate kettles, our private tables
and knives, and line up the bounty,
deciding which ones go where.
A canned peach, says one aunt, lasts ten years.
She was 87 last week. But a frozen peach
tastes better on ice cream.
Everything we have learned so far,
skins alive and ripening, on a day
that was real to us, that was summer,
motion going out and memory coming in.

1980

AND THESE SIGNS SHALL FOLLOW   121.
THEM THAT BELIEVE
MARK 16:17
Jan Epton Seale

Eyes that have tracked rabbits, birds, deer
all afternoon across the simple oak
now tear and smart, ready as they are
to discover in the cold Hill Country night
Orion among the hot uncompromising stars.

The astronomer emerges from his lens.
"We have a treat tonight," my son says
and waits until a plane has closed its path.
"First you find Orion by his belt."
His finger points me to the spangled girth.

And then we telescope the Great Hunter:
the yellow-red on his right shoulder named

Betelgeuse, a pulsing variable giant,
and Bellatrix on his left; straight down
find Rigel, making his knee a blue-white glint.

We shiver and our breaths form nebulae
of no order. "The next stars"—my son smiles —
"we'll see together. I have to show you how."
I *will* to see beyond the late-night books,
the fog of years, the dimming earthly weather.

"Beside the sword you'll see a cloudy mass."
I strain through waves and jerks from here to there,
search Orion's skirt for starry soil.
The cloud mass finally settles to its place.
"You mean the thing that looks like printers' dots?"

"Orion's Nebula," the astronomer says,
then stands against me firm to make a brace.
"Keep looking, Mom. For now, just blink and stare.
I promise you will see them if you try,
and hope—yes, hope for three bright stars."

Minutes go by. The click of the telescope timer
corrects what we cannot—our restless ride
on this galloping star-drenched porch.
And then the gift: three clear and perfect points,
three diamond apples where none were before.

Afraid to blink, I whisper, "Yes, I see them.
Yes." The astronomer's hand tightens on my arm.
"The Trapezium Cluster, at fifteen-hundred light-years."
He laughs. "I give them to you because you see them."
"I take them," I say, and feel him near.

2005

COMING THROUGH THE HILL COUNTRY: 122.
ON MY WAY BACK TO
SAN ANTONIO
Marian Haddad

They have cut through this
mountain of limestone rock—
21 miles from Ozona heading
east — made a way for us —
semis smoking — pipesmoke
charring chrome —
18 wheels roll alongside me —
I step on the gas — pass a Ballard sign
on the slate blue cab of the semi-
truck — it is 6 o'clock
and the streets are hot —
pavement thick
with heat,
and I'm driving faster now — I roll
the windows down as long as I can —
the air is hot — its damp heat
brushes my skin. This unbearable heat
is somehow sweet — though I must raise
the windows up — until the heat has passed —
chilled a bit — a degree — or two —
or ten — the sun will come
on this two-lane road they call
a highway — 1-10 East — coming
home — I should hit Sonora
before dusk, maybe catch
the sunset in my rearview —
over the mountains,

head on in through
that clear light
I expect.

2007

123. ALAMO PLAZA AT NIGHT
Carol Coffee Reposa

Even now, tourists come
To gaze up at the chipped façade,
Weathered double doors
Oaks twisting into dark, floodlights
Trained along their branches.
Cameras flash against white limestone
Pocked with centuries
And gunshots long ago.

Within the walls
And Roman arches
Heavy with their bars
Are tidy gardens:
Boston fern droops languidly
Toward fresh-cut grass
and copper plants.
Goldfish wallow in their quiet ponds.

Outside people talk about the mission,
Where to go, what to eat.
Visitors brood over maps
And time-lapse shots, children peering
At old plaques, words lost
Within a diesel's whine, the clop-clop

Of a horse's hooves, wind rising
In dark trees, voices gathered
Finally
Into the stones.

2002

"HEALTH CARE" THE SIGN SAYS   124.
Carmen Tafolla

From where I sit
in a car on the highway back
from the border,
entering this city that flows
through my soul
like a river too dark and green to be anything
but just what it is,
The Taco Cabana sign
stands taller than the Tower of the Americas.

I'd tried to explain
to the tourist at the convention center
last week
how the river is ours,
our property, our deed and title,
personal wealth,
even though we sweat each month
to pay the rent
or be evicted
and sometimes
are.
But you cross the river and the underbrush
at city limits barely fifteen minutes from the city's center
and see nothing,

no sign of civilization's mark from the last two
or three
centuries
except for the very highway you are on.
And then, like San Antonio itself,
civilization surprises you,
appears full-grown and looking at you straight
with God's Eyes, honest, painful, asking questions,
as buildings meant to be
our epitome and strength
appear.

You blinked
or turned away,
dozed off a second
and here we are in the middle of downtown
still going way too crazy-highway-fast
past hospitals, hotels as high,
and office-building-shadows-trends gone by.

"Health Care" the sign says
as I drive
but "No one cares"
unless you're wrapped in a green dollar bill
although the old part of the hospital still stands
and creaks and sighs
while arthritis attacks its legs.

The angel spreads her Vietnam Veteran wings
over a small child with a sick dove
despite protests to make her a Virgin,
especially in a Catholic hospital like this,
more cultural, traditional,
less prone to New Age healing fads, they recommend.

Off the highway now and we are here.
"Follow only new green highway signs"
the police officer tells us
"That way you'll get where you are going."
We do not listen well.
That is how we have gotten
this far.

Orphaned by all the others,
we do not stand alone.

the river pays the rent for us.
We are her deed
and title.

2001

THE LOST PARROT   125.
Naomi Shihab Nye

Carlos bites the end of his pencil
He's trying to write a dream-poem, but waves at me, frowning

     I had a parrot

He talks slowly, his voice travels far
to get out of his body

     a dream-parrot?
     No, a real parrot!
     Write about it

He squirms, looks nervous, everyone else is almost finished
and he hasn't started

It left
What left?
The *parrot*

He hunches over the table, pencil gripped in fist,
shaping the heavy letters
Days later we will write story-poems, sound-poems,
but always the same subject for Carlos.

It left.

He will insist on reading it and the class will look puzzled
The class is tired of this parrot

Write more, Carlos
I can't

Why not?

I don't know   where   it went

Each day when I leave he stares at the ceiling
Maybe he is planning an expedition
into the back streets of San Antonio
armed with nets and ripe mangoes
He will find the parrot nesting in a rain gutter
This time he will guard it carefully, make sure it stays

Before winter comes and his paper goes white
in all directions

Before anything else he loves
gets away

1982

DRIVING TOWARD HOUSTON 126.
Paul Christensen

The miles are more like time than anything—
disks of prairie turning
like clocks in either window
in each of them a cow stands
or a horse nods itself to sleep
a house darkens against the distance
We are the present moment tangible as
breeze but no more, shifting the boundary
between east and west, this crumbling wall
of north behind us, sealing as we move
into the dissolving south, its unmade history
gushing like springs before us

1999

KUDZU 127.
Larry D. Thomas

Near downtown Houston, in my own
garden, its lithe, relentless stems
wrap the limbs of my mountain laurel
and speed toward its crown
like thin, green boas
tightening their grip for the kill.
It grows so fast in the South

one who watches it intently,
only for minutes,
can easily see it move,
like these tendrils it sprouted
in the vacant lot next-door,
slithering this very minute
beneath my patio fence,

invading the brick floor
right before my eyes
and heading for my sliding
glass door like silent green cracks
growing wider by the second,
reclaiming as wilderness
what I only thought was mine.

2007

128.

TEXAS SPLENDOR
Janet Lowery

Here in Houston there's no stomach for misery.
That brilliant sun, that curtain of heat indexes
and barometric sweat, those glistening ladies,
those cowboy hats and silver belts and studded spurs
decorating very young old men, those long days
in which the light goes on forever, the hills
flattened, the sky perpetually bright,
and the homeless, the street people panhandling
like smiling buffoons at traffic stop circuses,
like artifacts of wisdom, like pointillist dots
of brown and grey in a landscape of blue glass
and bougainvillea. Here in Houston we remember
there will be poor always and guys who work downtown
tell you bitterly those bums in front of the courthouse
pull in two hundred a day, but anyway, not everyone
can be rich and those who are not live some place
farther north or turn against themselves
in selfish anorexic fits or bouts of cocaine use.
Help is cheap. The barrios sleep, quaint and
dark in distant neighborhoods and even I can not
sustain a complaint, so determined are those around me,
so confident are they of standing ground in the nation

of Texas and besides, who can resist the profusion
of spangled palms at Christmastide, the valet-parking
shopping marts, the rhinestone vests and sequin dresses
suggesting we sparkle our glittered way across
the two-step double-turn neon-lit western-swing
dance floor into a heaven where Stevie Ray
and Reba's band and Daniel Boone and Davy Crockett
and all the other heroes of the country western rock-n-roll
Alamo wait for us in radiant Texas splendor.

1994

CERELLE
Margaret Belle Houston

129.

THERE was a score of likely girls
Around the prairieside,
But I went down to Galveston
And brought me home a bride.

A score or more of handsome girls,
Of proper age and size,
But the pale girls of Galveston
Have sea-shine in their eyes.

As pale as any orange flower,
Cerelle. The gold-white sands
Were like her hair, and drifting shells,
White fairy shells, her hands.

I think she liked my silver spurs,
A-clinking in the sun.
She'd never seen a cowboy till
I rode to Galveston.

She'd never known the chaparral,
Nor smell of saddle leather,
Nor seen a round-up or a ranch,
Till we rode back together.

Shall I forget my mother's eyes?
"Is this the wife you need?
Is this the way to bring me rest
From forty men to feed?"

Cerelle—I think she did her best
All year. She'd lots to learn.
Dishes would slip from out her hands
And break. The bread would burn.

And she would steal away at times
And wander off to me.
And when the wind was in the south
She'd say, "I smell the sea!"

She changed. The white and gold grew dull
As when a soft flame dies,
And yet she kept until the last
The sea-shine in her eyes.

There are (I make a husband's boast)
No stronger arms than Ann's.
She has a quip for all the boys,
And sings among the pans.

At last my mother takes her rest.
And that's how things should be.
but when the wind is in the south
There is no rest for me.

1930

ON THE PATIO, DALLAS 130.
Isabel Nathaniel

The prickly pear and yucca
dug from a roadside
do fine in pots. Sun,
sunflowers. The August heat.
Petunias, pinks, and even the geranium
probably don't belong. With watering
they hold on. One morning
I fed them Ortho Fertilizer
made entirely of sea-going fish.
I hosed the place till
the hanging baskets dripped
and the fence soaked dark.
There rose the brackish
smell of bays and wharves
and I turned my head
to the distance as if to hear
the regular slapping of the sea.

Isabel Nathaniel

1995

TO A DALLAS LADY 131.
Lawrence Chittenden

I SING this song to one who long
Has charmed me with a spell;
A lady who has blessed my life
Far more than I can tell.
'Twere vain to try, I cannot gauge,
Her charms in feeble measures,
For, oh, her mind and soul refined
Are rich in mental treasures.

Her song, with smiles, all care beguiles,
  To her the pow'r is given
To gild all weary hearts with joy,
  And make this earth a heaven.

She is a garland of delight,
  A queen of royal manner,
A wreath of flowers from Southern bowers
  From fair Louisiana.

Ah, yes! she's kind, you'll always find
  Her heart is free from malice,
She seems ideal, but yet she's real,
  This lady lives in Dallas.
This song I send to her, my friend,
  The loveliest of the sexes,
Long may she live to bless the world
  And reign a Queen of Texas.
1893

132.   DALLAS
                          Dave Oliphant

encircled by freeway loops
has wished itself a Roman arena
styled more after Texas Stadium
where gladiators   this time
Christians from Abilene or SMU
take on Lions Bears Rams
while the lawyer-merchant class
spies down night & day
from box seats or tinted glass
spots the animals in goal-line stands
or last ditches along skidrow

below
too are those looking for history   staring at tobacco stains on
Federal Building walks   visitors in from Boston
wondering
Is this where our hero bled?
buying his souvenirs   windows Xed
in snapshots where Oswald took his aim
his bullet granting one more wish

such carpet rides lift powerlines
overpasses skyscrapers high
rises hopes of masses   recall
how they were raised for
days   driving here as a family when fall
trips to the State Fair were long & hard
where at last in Sears would try
the cowboy boots had wanted so   like Gene's
or Roy's but with narrow feet
dad said no   they didn't fit
nothing in Dallas ever does
it's Texas but then it's not
it isn't the West it never was
would have it moved to an eastern spot

partly this comes out as
the talk of a Cowtown boy   Fort Worth-Dallas
called twin cities yet rivals from the start
the real Texas   with cattle & horses
rodeos at Will Rogers Coliseum   versus
the Airport

typical of towns grown near   the closest father & son
are born to carry a rivalry on
          Darío's red head sticks

Dave Oliphant

out in any crowd
can be a pain   yet will claim him any time
like all of Texas   or so would rhyme

Big D's a sore thumb too
though giving credit where credit's due
both share winning points
this city can boast of parks & lakes
are a blue-green sketch
for him to sit & draw   match
with watercolor or tempera paints
outdo this description   make a papa proud

carry him back to creeks shaded
by pecan & peach   running clear & cold
over smooth & green-furred rocks   fresh
by willows   in summer a cool conversing   traded
for memos typed at the Apparel Mart   to baskets sold
beside the bridge   their priceless wrinkled pits
brown-black nuts fallen at feet once bared to ripples   rainbow perch   a movement Darío can better catch

need for that his art   need his love
needed Love Field too   a where to land
& seek for him athletic fun   a higher
flight than had on fleetest jets   a swimming hole for deeper dives than
dips on tollway drives   a where to buy
western boots for the skinny kid
right for walking streets can still recov-
er that magic word will trim shed blood
like a genii whisped
back inside an olympic
lamp overrubbed

1976

ON THE PORCH—DENTON, TEXAS   133.

Martha Elizabeth

Let us live the slow way,
watching the light
while the rail-posts shadow us
with lengthening stripes.
The hours have our own momentum, a pace
logical as cloth.
Fossils from a local creek,
and stones from travels, unpolished.
Cowskull, cholla skeleton.
An oak stump, partly hollow,
where a glass leaves rings.

No more movement than to lift a wet glass.
Skin glossed with sweat.
Cool shininess
like a mirror glancing back at the sun.

Let us turn the rule of time
to pleasure, the hours
measured by design,
tailored for fullness.

Taillights blaze and dim
to the west horizon avenue.
A wasp returns to the stump and enters it,
filling the hole where the heart was,
making itself at home.

1995

Martha Elizabeth

134.

NACOGDOCHES SPEAKS
Karle Wilson Baker

I was The Gateway. Here they came and passed,
The homespun centaurs with their arms of steel
And taut heart-strings: wild wills, who thought to deal
Bare-handed with jade Fortune, tracked at last
Out of her silken lairs into the vast
Of a man's world. They passed, but still I feel
The dent of hoof, the print of booted heel,
Like prick of spurs—the shadows that they cast.

I do not vaunt their valors, or their crimes:
I tell my secrets only to some lover,
Some taster of spilled wine and scattered musk.
But I have not forgotten; and, sometimes,
The things that I remember rise, and hover
A sharper perfume, in some April dusk.

1929

135.

BIG THICKET WORDS
James Marion Cody

Full Moon
Rises
over tops
of Pines.
Yellow
from the red
left
by the Sun
just passed

clear
from the woods
on our right
from the car.
In the East
Ikemetubbe
rising
from the fog
over the lake.
White
Sky.

1976

HOW THE BIG THICKET GOT SMALLER   136.
Jerry Bradley

First they got the panther,
then the bear.
The pigeon flocks
went with the wild timber,
and oil,
plain crude,
drove out dens of all sorts.
Roads did in the plants.

There are still some trees
though now they stand
in a slaughterhouse of saws,
and iron rigs,
black as poachers' kettles,
bob like chained birds
drinking from the earth.

Jerry Bradley

181

A life ordered and lubed,
hard as blacktop,
a tax supported legacy
for the mechanical world
where the ivorybill
once tapped its confused code
and big cats screamed
like frightened women in the dark.

1991

ONE ATTEMPT AT DEFINING TEXANS

LONG GONE TO TEXAS 137.
William D. Barney

Some of those pioneers who came
out of dead hopes, unevened scores,
wrote three stark letters on their doors,
shook disappointment off, and shame,
and headed here to kindle a new star.

At twelve I had no lasting hurt,
no stricken heart, no dream's debris.
Transplanted like an up-plucked tree,
my roots caught into splendid dirt,
and soon reset the running calendar.

Whoever cultivates this patch
earth color will stick to his hand.
Gladly I gather from this land
whatever harvest I can scratch.
The field, like the star, is large and singular.

Add one more letter to the three.
I'll carve the legend on my bark,
a culminating brand to mark
more than a half of century—
Long Gone to Texas. Here my horizons are.

1986

138.   TEXAS
                          William Allen Ward

Texas,
Child of the West,
Who talks in the soft voice
Of the South, but packs a gun
On his hip.

Texas,
A two-gun killer
Who looks the gambling cheat
Straight in the eye—a pistol bark…
Then death!

Texas,
A rowdy boy,
With the wind for a pal
And the sunset to paint his cheeks
With health.

Texas,
A little girl,
Who plucks a wild flower
On the hill of June, to put in
Her hair.

1934

THE REAL AMERICA 139.
Red Steagall

I've traveled 'cross this country, been in towns from coast
  to coast,
Played rodeos and clubs and county fairs.
I look for my America in every place I go.
I find her where her people truly care.

I found her in San Angelo at old Ft. Concho Days,
At Copper Mountain Westfest in the fall,
In Winchester, Virginia, during apple blossom time,
In Cheyenne at the granddad of them all.

It's not impressive buildings or the car the mayor drives.
It's people in her towns that make her tall.
It's caring for each other, being quick to lend a hand,
The pride in people down at city hall.

The Western Heritage Classic in the town of Abilene
Is one that stole my cowboy heart away.
The spirit and the values upon which this country stands
Are things I saw in Abilene today.

While walking down the thoroughfare amongst the
  milling throng,
Where western wear is more than just a fad,
I saw the little fellers in their cowboy hats and boots
Tryin' hard to walk and talk just like their dads.

Then down in the arena, all the teams were recognized.
Each cowboy's proud he's riding for the brand.
He's keen to competition and is loyal to the core,
But always first to lend a helping hand.

When they played the national anthem, every person
   faced the flag.
With hats in hand they sang their souls away.
My heart welled up inside me as I listened to them sing.
I heard the real America today.

The ones who built this country must have been this
   kind of folks
No envy, spite or pride gets in the way;
Respect for other people, bein' proud of who you are—
Perhaps the world will understand someday.

The backbone of this country is the folks who work
   the land
Like raisin' stock or growin' wheat and corn.
They learn responsibility before they learn to walk.
Friends, this is where America is born.

Integrity and honesty are what they teach their young.
You have a chance, be all you dare to be.
I saw no guns or violence, heard no insults, threats or lies—
Just people bein' happy, livin' free.

They have their share of problems, but they face them
   with a smile,
They live life in a simple kind of way.
They dream of a tomorrow, with respect for yesteryear.
I saw the real America today.

1994

A TRUE TEXAN
Peggy Zuleika Lynch

140.

A true Texan wears the Lone Star in his heart
as well as over it.
A true Texan matches his valor
against anyone's at the drop of a hat.
A true Texan clings to his land
not as landed gentry
but as gentle to the land.

It's his domain.
It's his kingdom.
Out of the sand, the brush, the cacti, the mesquite,
the plush metropolitan cities
wherever the Lone Star flies,
the people who are truly Texan vie and defy
the rugged tornadoes, the demolishing floods
the burning droughts, the inexplicable crime.
They take what comes
and stretch the mind
to weather fortune's decree:
true men of grit.
(Chorus)
    We are Texas rugged individualists.
   We can live in a hovel
         or live in a palace.
     It makes no great difference
       and we have no malice.
We're game to whatever destiny deals us
      YES, WE ARE TEXANS;
        the nation loves us?
We are fundamentally antagonists

to whatever "out does" us!
We just go on and buck up!
YES, WE ARE TEXAS RUGGED INDIVIDUALISTS.
WE'RE TEXANS!
The nation loves us?

1980

141.   ALL THE OLD SONGS
                        Walter McDonald

I never knew them all, just hummed
and thrummed my fingers with the radio,
driving a thousand miles to Austin.
Her arms held all the songs I needed.
Our boots kept time with fiddles
and the charming sobs of blondes,

the whine of steel guitars
sliding us down in deer-hide chairs
when jukebox music was over.
Sad music's on my mind tonight
in a jet high over Dallas, earphones
on channel five. A lonely singer,

dead, comes back to beg me,
swearing in my ears she's mine,
rhymes set to music which make
complaints seem true. She's gone
and others like her, leaving their songs
to haunt us. Letting down through clouds

I know who I'll find tonight at home,
the same woman faithful to my arms
as she was those nights in Austin
when the world seemed like a jukebox,
our boots able to dance forever,
our pockets full of coins.

1993

LITANY: BLOOD IN THE SOIL/TEXAS   142.
(an excerpt)
sharon bridgforth

i
am
the child
of the daughter of a
just-waxed-Moon gurl   who
birthed the African
that jumped ship
and flew back home
to seek him Ancestors
guard his seed   destined
to walk through
the door of no return
into the arms of slavery/i am
the gran-granny's/daughter
of the wo'mn
guided to the Indigenous Chief that
took her people in to safety/i have
blood memories of
the Red Road
and the African Way

sharon bridgforth

i can hear the drum
but can't recall the chant/i
no longer know the cry of names
that proceeded me/i am
trying to remember
Harriet Tubman
Frederick Douglass
i am trying
Old Gran Nanny
Black Elk
to remember
Tituba
Marie LaVeau
i am trying
Martin Luther King
Barbara Jordan
to remember
Fannie Lou Hamer
Ceasar Chavez
i m listening
Langston Hughes
      Audre Lorde
and
Praying
Yemonja
Tequantla
Mother of God
Keeper of the Waters of Life
OH MIGHTY AND DIVINE GUARDIAN SPIRITS
WHO'VE GONE BEFORE
WHO PAVED THE WAY
WHO BLESS US NOW
have mercy
HOLY AND SACRED ONES
protect us and lead the way

i am
WE
sitting in the Sun
waiting
for the Moon
to come back
and carry
Us
Home.

i am
standing
firm-footed
in the
Blood of my people.

2006

OUR TEXAS ECONOMY   143.
Chuck Taylor

seems like every boy I know
has been cut back or laid off—
or the business they run
ain't got no business

Larry's moved in with his mom
and sold his 'Vet;
Kim is talking about
reconciling with her old man.
they've been separated a year.
"I just can't support these kids
on my own," she says
why, high tech got so high—

Chuck Taylor

eight miles high they say—
that it just rides the jet stream
from California to Boston,
back and forth
back and forth,
missing Texas

And crude oil got so plentifully crude
it's almost oozing out of the floorboards.
I heard a chemist talking
of converting the stuff
to synthetic chocolate

But don't despair
with the coming cold of December.
Your lover's eyes
are just as warm as ever
and a kiss is still a kiss,
guaranteeing higher yield
than a jumbo CD

and goodness—oh yes goodness—
it's painted all over the asphalt,
all over homes and buildings
just like it always was.
goodness, your best investment,
that outlasts all greed
and all the pennies of despair

1986

AQUÍ
Carmen Tafolla

144.

He wanders through the crooked streets
that mimic river beds Before,
and breathes the anxious air in traffic
filled with tension left from wooded crossroads in attack.
He shops the windows, happy,
where the stalking once was good,
and his kitchen floor is built on bones
of venison once gently roasted.

"It's a good place for a party!" he concurs
to friends now dressed in jeans.

The ground was already beaten smooth
and festive by the joy of ancient dances.

He feels the warmth,
and doesn't know his soul is filled
with the spirit of coyotes past.

1993

PECOS BILL IN DECLINE
Steve Harrigan

145.

A disease has attacked
the plumage of his chaps.
He sheds in the parlor
while the ladies feel his muscle.

All that fluff and fur, that dream:
a grizzly cub nuzzling him down

into the secret corners of his crib;
the desert; a sky filled with
ice and minerals;

the cold nose of his coyote mother
and her wide-set eyes
stunned with love.

Before the mirror
he sees his bare legs bowed
like railroad ties.

It has been long time
since he has lassoed a train
or the far bank of a river.
But trust him: he may yet
bury his face in the grasslands.

He may take up the state of Texas
and wear its hide
next to his skin.

1980

146.

STILTS AND OTHER VEHICLES
Richard Sale

The old masters posed themselves at a window,
Forearm along the sill to form a base.
From that vantage they could view the world.
I learned to walk in Sweetwater, Tex.
In Athens, next, I got good enough on them
To climb the high steps of the First Baptist Church.

Then on to Palestine, to fence balancing,
To Corpus Christi, to surfboards, filled glasses
On a bent arm. Classical names, classical poses.

Now I have walked on my Western stilts
In London, Paris, Seville, standing on one foot
In awe and a self-conscious perversity of pride.
I may progress to some exotic Polynesian posture before
it's over.
The High Plains and Piney Woods and the low
Dunes of the coastal flats are far behind.
But a jingling spur: What you thought you outgrew
Shaped whatever gait you've grown into.

Richard Sale

1978

147.

SPELL MY NAME

Teresa Paloma Acosta

My name is Cristina Lopez Gonzalez.
That's Cristina without the h
And Gonzalez with an s.
(Here a shrug.)

Yo me llamo Josefina Paulette Gomez,
And there's an accent mark
On the o in Gomez
But we don't use it
(Here a smile and a tilt of the head toward me.)

I'm Pedro. Last name Rodriguez, which is w-aay
too largo for me. But I'll give it a try.
(Here a concentrated frown, pencil midair.)

I'm Nico—well, Nicolás;
that's the English say of saying it
and the Spanish way of spelling.
(Here a broad grin.)

Question: Nico, Do you like it that way?
Answer: Well, yeah.
My 'buela insists on the Spanish version.
Question: Nico, what do you like?
(Here a shrug and a "both.")

I mind my 'buela. If she says it in Spanish,
I say it's a-ok with me.
(Here a spontaneous "Nicolás"
como en Spanish.)

Here the mark of Tex-Mex is
on every tongue/lengua franca.
Y no importa que digan los jefes,
who bend over the Spanish
dictionary, counting every missed syllable.

2003

148.

OUR SPEAKER THIS MORNING
Chris Willerton

If you come early to one of these little churches,
there's nobody but you and the midmorning
summerlight, thunk of your car door,
crunch of gravel as you walk watching
strands of yellow grass tap the wooden porch.
The door is never locked, the bathroom

never has towels.
You may or may not find a map
of The Divided Kingdom, among dusty
Vacation Bible School projects.
Since the placid class may or may not remember what
the regular man said last week about Solomon,
prepare an extra scripture, an extra illustration
about dictators. You may need it to even up
the portion of wisdom.

Whenever they come, family at a time,
in pickups or five-year-old sedans,
you clutch for names, remark
the need for rain, squint
past at the sidewalk and hope for fifteen
or twenty. Mount to the speaker's stand
and the banks of the Jordan,
painted above the dry baptistery.

Chris Willerton

Someone leads a hymn, then you just
teach. Fifteen faces among fifty seats
in a forty-year-old frame building
aren't a threat. They've seen better teachers
and much worse. At the worship service
don't worry either. Sufficient unto the day
is the guest preacher thereof. They've
put up with nineteen-year-old preaching-students,
yammering missionaries, mumbling profs
who haven't preached fulltime in years.
These folk know charity. There isn't much
you could tell them anyway.

Don't go out to preach unless you want to.
On the hour's drive out, your only companions are
fenceline hawks and Herefords, dead armadillos, and

(angels in dark glasses)
the Texas Department of Public Safety.
The radio has only county/ western whining
or gospel bellowing. And whoever's turn it is
may take you home to fried chicken and okra
or tough leftover pork roast and shrunken peas.

I'll tell you really why you go:
gradually the people turn into brethren.
Old Bennie Sanders hates the liberals;
get him to talk instead
about his fifty-four gray Studebaker truck
or his grandson playing basketball in college
or his leading songs, before his emphysema came.
Get Maude to show you butterbeans she put up.
Sympathize on the cost of her eight medicines
and the red tape with Medicare.
While she puts ice cream on the peaches,
look out the window at the grain elevator
and neighbor's brick house that weren't there
when Bennie set the window in.

After the evening service you won't have
any trouble thanking them.
They used to have sixty members,
now have twenty. And the kids
keep growing up and moving away.

1983

IF I COULDN'T GET TO THE RIVER 149.
Steven Fromholz

If I couldn't get to the river
I reckon I would surely die.
The river can give a man reason to live
When the rest of the world says, "Why?"
If you're lookin' for somethin' that delivers
Come on give the river a try,
We can sit on the bank
Let our minds go blank
And let the rest of the world go by.

Steven Fromholz

If I couldn't get to the canyon
I wouldn't have no place to go.
I love that ditch, Lord, I'd be rich
If I hadn't learned how to row that boat
But she made me a true companion
One night 'neath the full moon's glow
Now the stars that shine in the night are mine
As I rest by the old Bravo.

And if I can't get to my baby
There's gonna be hell to pay
And I pity the man who makes his plan
To get in this ol' boy's way.
Ain't no ifs or ands or maybes 'bout anything that I say.
She's my lovin' friend 'till the livin' end
Gonna see my baby today.

And if I can't get to the desert
You know the desert gonna come get me
It'll slip into town, all dusty and brown,
Come lookin' for the refugee.
Running with the desert is a pleasure

Always took the measure of me
And if you're lookin' around
And I can't be found
Well, the desert is where I'll be.

2001

150. AT THE SEVEN-MILE RANCH, COMSTOCK, TEXAS
Naomi Shihab Nye

I live like I know what I'm doing.

When I hand the horses a square of hay,
when I walk the road of stones
or chew on cactus pulp,
there's a drumming behind me,
the day opens up to let me pass through.

I know the truth,
how always I'm following each small sign that appears.
This sheep that materialized behind a clump of cenizo bushes
knows I didn't see him till he raised his head.

Out here it's impossible to be lonely.
The land walking beside you is your oldest friend,
pleasantly silent, like already you've told the best stories
and each of you knows how much the other made up.

1982

THE POETS

TERESA PALOMO ACOSTA was born in McGregor in Central Texas and now lives in Austin. Her poetry collections are *Passing Time, Nile and Other Poems,* and *In the Season of Change.* In 2003, the historian and poet co-wrote with Ruthe Winegarten, *Las Tejanas: 300 Years of History* (The University of Texas Press). *The New Handbook of Texas* includes her entries on Hispanic life (The Texas State Historical Association). Acosta's writings have appeared in *New Texas 93, An Anthology of Chicana Literature,* and *United States in Literature.* Teresa Palomo Acosta is a direct descendant of the Maximino Palomo of the poem in this anthology.

KARLE WILSON BAKER, author of nine books of prose and poetry, was one the first Texans to reach a national readership. Baker was published in *Century, Atlantic Monthly, Scribner's,* and *Best Poems of 1923, English and American.* Her 1931 poetry collection, *Dreamers on Horseback,* was nominated for a Pulitzer Prize. She was a charter member of the Texas Institute of Letters (the only woman). Between 1924 and 1934, Karle Wilson Baker was an English professor at Stephen F. Austin State Teacher's College in Nacogdoches.

WILLIAM D. BARNEY was a Fort Worth postal inspector and an American poet. He was one of the first Texas poets to lend concrete images and precise language to Texas subjects. Critic Paul Christensen describes the Fort Worth poet: "Barney is the first writer of real size to drive the New England poem west and make it register the life of the Southwest." William D. Barney received the Robert Frost Award presented in New York City. During the ceremony, Robert Frost himself presented the Fort Worth poet with the award. Two of Barney's books are recipients of Texas Institute of Letters poetry awards. His best collection, *The Killdeer Crying,* was published by Prickly Pear Press, and his last collection, *A Cowtown Chronicle,* was published by Browder Springs Press. The late William D. Barney served as Texas Poet Laureate, 1982–1983.

PRESTON P. BATEMAN contributed to *Texas Poems,* an anthology that he also published. This poem shows the enthusiastic attitude of the Texas populace toward the celebrations of our Centennial Year of 1936. Bateman managed a Tyler school supply and publishing company, through which he furthered his passion for verse. In 1936, many Texas students recited Bateman's patriotic poems, "Our Flag" and "Our Centennial!"

ALAN BIRKELBACH is a computer analyst as well as the 2005 Texas Poet Laureate. *Bone Song* (1996), *No Boundaries* (1997), and *Weighed in the Balance* (1998) are three of his books. TCU Press recently published *Alan Birkelbach: New and Selected Poems,* the first publication in its TCU Texas Poet Laureate Series. A native of rural central Texas, Alan Birkelbach lives with his wife Laura in Plano.

MARGIE B. BOSWELL graduated from Texas Christian University. In the 1940s, she published prose and poetry in the *Fort Worth Star-Telegram* while teaching high-school English. "Girls of the Rodeo" comes from Boswell watching trick riders in the old Fort Worth Fat Stock Show.

JERRY BRADLEY is the author of the poetry book, *Simple Version of Disaster.* A member of the Texas Institute of Letters, he was the founding editor of the respected *New Mexico Humanities Review* and now serves as the poetry editor for *Concho River Review.* Today, Bradley is still a poet when not occupied by his vice-presidential duties at Lamar University in Beaumont.

SHARON BRIDGFORTH, visual artist and poet, mixes jazz rhythms and performance art with her poetics. Her award-winning writings have received funding from The National Endowment For the Arts and The Rockefeller Foundation. Bridgforth has placed individual pieces in literary publications, including *Kentecloth: Southwest Voices of the African Diaspora; !TEX!; Affirming Flame: Writing by Progressive Texas Poets in the Aftermath of September 11th;* and *Is This Forever, Or What?* The touring visual artist and writer has selected Austin as her home base.

In addition to editing and publishing with her imprint, *Plain View Press,* **SUSAN BRIGHT** is an award-winning poet. Bright has received a PEN Award and has worked in the Artist-In-Schools program. In connection with this book's "Riding the Currents" and her collection, *Breathing Under Water,* she has served as a board member of Save Barton Creek. Among her collections are *Far Side of the Word, Atomic Basket, Tirades and Evidence of Grace,* and *House of Mother,* with the last two receiving Austin Book Awards.

WILLIAM LAWRENCE CHITTENDEN was once widely known as "The Poet Ranchman." Larry, as he called himself in his stanzas, began writing while cowboying on his uncle's ranch along the Old Mackenzie Trails. After he inherited his uncle's property, Chittenden's book sales allowed him to expand the ranch's operations. *Ranch Verses* was first published 1893, and by Chittenden's death in 1934, the book had been reprinted fifteen times for an international readership.

PAUL CHRISTENSEN is an award-winning short story writer, poet, and a professor at Texas A&M University. He has published seven books of poetry, along with a body of literary criticism, including *West of the American Dream: An Encounter with Texas.* Christensen is a former NEA Poetry Fellow. He is a current member of the Texas Institute of Letters, and his short story "Water" received a Texas Institute of Letters award. His 2001 book of prose poems, *Blue Alleys,* received a Violet Crown award. His 2003 poetry collection is *Mottled Air.* Recently, Christensen co-edited with Rick Bass *Falling from Grace in Texas: A Literary Response to the Demise of Paradise.*

JAMES MARION CODY was an authority on Native America, an American literature scholar, small press publisher, and a published poet. Cody's legacy continues within the memories of those in the Texas literature scene who knew him and in his books of poetry. His titles are *Colorado River, Prayer to Fish, A Book of Wonders, Return, My Body Is A Flute,* and *Elvis, Immortality.*

BETSY FEAGAN COLQUITT edited the literary journal *descant*, the William D. Barney collection, *Cowtown Chronicle*, and the anthology, *A Part of Space: Ten Texas Writers.* Her first collection, *Honor Card*, is considered a classic. Scholar James Ward Lee says of her 1997 retrospective collection, *Eve*: "Good poetry makes the familiar seem new. True poetry must, as Pope says of true wit, tell us 'what oft was thought but ne'er so well expressed.' The poems of Betsy Colquitt's *Eve—from the Autobiography and Other Poems* do exactly that and more. Not only are the 'oft thought' things in Colquitt's poetry 'well expressed,' but the 'Eve' poems even offer new thoughts." Betsy Feagan Colquitt, a retired professor from Texas Christian University, lives in Fort Worth.

SARAH CORTEZ, besides working as a police officer, teaches creative writing at the University of Houston as a Visiting Scholar. She received a 1999 PEN Texas Literary Award, and her poem, "Glance," was featured by Houston's METRO buses as part of the national program, "Poetry in Motion." Her 1998 collection is *How To Undress a Cop.* Ms. Cortez is editing *Look Into My Window: Memoirs by Latino Youth*, forthcoming in 2007 from Arte Público Press. The two poems in this collection are from a book in progress.

JIM CRACK may have been a pseudonym. The period piece, "Farewell to Senator Sam Houston," was published on an 1849 editorial page, originally in *The Texas State Gazette* of Austin. Little is known about this opinion piece contributor, other than the included poem that criticizes the politics of Houston, while praising the man.

A. L. CROUCH, a Fort Worth lawyer, had degrees from Texas Christian University and the University of Texas at Austin. Crouch first wrote poetry and nonfiction while fighting in the Pacific Theater during World War II. "Mirabeau B. Lamar" was included in the anthology, *Where the West Begins.*

GRACE NOLL CROWELL, the author of thirty-five books of children stories, inspirational writings, and poetry, was a resident of Dallas. In 1925, her first book, *White Fire*, received awards in America and England. In sales, she is among the best-selling American poets of all time. The Poet Laureate of Texas, 1936–1939, she was a regular in such magazines as *Good Housekeeping, Christian Science Monitor, McCall's* and *New York Times.* The 1938 biographical publication, *American Women*, named Crowell one of Ten Outstanding Women in the United States. Her retrospective collection is *The Eternal Things: The Best of Grace Noll Crowell.*

NORMAN H. CROWELL, husband of Grace Noll Crowell, had his own accomplishments as a writer. *Field and Stream, The Saturday Evening Post*, and other well-known magazines of the 1940s and 1950s picked up his nonfiction and poetry.

WILLIAM V. DAVIS is the author of nine books of poetry and six volumes of literary criticism. Among his poetry collections are *One Way to Reconstruct the Scene* (Winner of the Yale Series of Younger Poets Award for 1979), *The Dark Hours,* and *Winter Light.* He is Writer-in-Residence at Baylor University.

MARTHA ELIZABETH, formerly of Austin and Denton, received a number of recognitions, including a Dobie Paisano Fellowship. Her poems have been selected for publication in such publications as *New Texas, New England Review,* and *Blue Mesa Review.* Martha Elizabeth now lives Missoula, Montana. Her award-winning book, *Return of Pleasure,* was published in 1995 by Confluence Press.

ROBERT A. FINK, who served in the Vietnam War, is the W.D. and Hollis R. Bond Professor of English at Hardin-Simmons University in Abilene. His poetry often delineates the interaction between the land of West Texas and its people. The member of the Texas Institute of Letters had two books published in 2006: his fifth collection of poetry, *Tracking the Morning,* and a literary nonfiction book, *Twilight Innings: A West Texan on Grace and Survival.*

STEVEN FROMHOLZ actor, songwriter, and poet. Best known as the composer of such songs as "The Man in the Big Hat" and "Texas Trilogy," he is the 2007 Texas Poet Laureate. In addition, he is also known for leading canoe trips; *Paddler Magazine* called Fromholz, "one of the best river guides in America." Fromholz, in between performances, continues to write poetry.

EDWARD H. GARCIA originally of Brownsville, Texas, for some time has been a professor of writing and literature at Brookhaven College in Dallas. His reviews, short fiction, and poetry have been included in literary publications, including *The Texas Humanist, Texas Observer, Pawn Review, Texas Short Stories II,* and *New Texas 2000.* Garcia spends summer and weekends enjoying the quiet life with his wife in East Texas, where he intends to retire.

MARIAN HADDAD, poet and essayist, was born to Syrian immigrants in El Paso. Haddad has an MFA in Creative Writing from San Diego State University, and she was a recipient of an NEA endowment. Her 2003 chapbook of poems, *Saturn Falling Down,* was compiled under the request of Texas Public Radio. Marian Haddad's 2004 full-length book of poems, *Somewhere between Mexico and a River Called Home,* was recommended by *The Small Press Review.* Her works in progress are evolving into two collections of poetry and one of personal essays on growing up Arab-American in a Mexican-American border town.

STEPHEN HARRIGAN is a poet, screenwriter, journalist, and novelist. He grew up in Abilene and Corpus Christi and lives in Austin. Among the movies that he has written for television are TNT's *King of Texas* and HBO's *The Last of His Tribe.* A former staff writer at *Texas Monthly,* Harrigan has had his prose published in *Aububon, The Atlantic,* and *Life.* His two nonfiction books are *A Natural State* and *Comanche Midnight.* His first two novels, *Aransas* and *Jacob's Well,* were critically acclaimed. His third, *The Gates of the Alamo,* became a *New York Times* bestseller and received a number of honors, including the TCU Book Award, the Western Heritage Award from the National Cowboy and Western Heritage Museum, and the Spur Award for the Best Western Novel of the West. Stephen Harrigan's fourth novel, *Challenger Park,* is set at the NASA facility in Texas. Harrigan's only book of poetry, *Sleepyhead,* is a good read, too.

CLYDE WALTON HILL, a Dallas high-school teacher of English, wrote poetry that appeared in *The Christian Science Monitor, The Literary Digest,* and *The Saturday Evening Post.* His 1926 book of poems, *Shining Trails,* contains "Little Towns of Texas."

ROLANDO HINOJOSA-SMITH teaches creative writing at the University of Texas at Austin. Critic Tom Pilkington states: "The most prolific contemporary Texas Mexican writer is Rolando Hinojosa." The South Texas native is famous for his *Klail City Death Trip Series,* which consists of short fiction, poems, and novels. His novel in this series, *The Valley,* won the internationally coveted Casa de las Americas Award. In 2006, Arte Publico Press released *We Happy Few,* Hinojosa-Smith's most recent depiction of Mexican-American life in the Valley.

JAMES HOGGARD and his wife Lynn live in a Wichita Falls house originally built by a magician. For years, James Hoggard has taught at Midwestern State University. Hoggard, the 2000 Texas Poet Laureate, has authored seventeen books—of poetry, nonfiction, novels, and translations. He was the recipient of the 1990 Texas Institute of Letters Award in short story. Hoggard's body of work also contains his 2003 collection of short stories, *Patterns of Illusion,* and the 2005 book of poems, *Wearing the River.*

MARY AUSTIN HOLLEY was a first cousin of Stephen F. Austin. After the Republic of Texas was established, the teacher and writer acted as an unofficial ambassador to the United States, especially in her writings urging Texas annexation. Born in New Haven, Connecticut, she died in New Orleans. Her first two trips to Texas—in 1831 and in 1835—resulted in widely read publications. She is remembered for *Texas: Observations, Historical, Geographical, and Descriptive, in a Series of Letters Written during a Visit to Austin's Colony, with a View to a Permanent Settlement during a Visit to Austin's Colony in the Autumn of 1831* (published 1833) and *Texas* (1836). *Texas* is the first history of our state written in English. She visited her Texas estate again in the 1840s. Her pencil sketches, family letters, and diary entries are also a state cultural legacy.

BOYCE HOUSE was a staff reporter with the *Fort Worth Star-Telegram,* where he wrote the syndicated column, "I Give You Texas." He also worked in Hollywood as a technical advisor for "Texas" movies before unsuccessfully running for lieutenant governor of this state. He is remembered as a popular humorist. His only book of poetry, *Texas Rhythm and Other Poems,* was published in 1950.

MARGARET BELLE (BELL) HOUSTON, poet and novelist, was the granddaughter of legendary Sam Houston. In some of her publications, her middle name is given as "Belle," in others, "Bell." In the 1920s and 1930s, her poetry was published in such magazines as *Good Housekeeping, Harpers,* and *McCalls.*

SAMUEL HOUSTON, twice president of the Republic of Texas and the first U.S. Senator from Texas, is recognized for his political accomplishments—like being the only person to be a governor of two different U.S. states (first Tennessee, then Texas)—but not for his dabbling in poetry. Like many gentlemen of his day, he versified as a pastime. His "Texian Call to Arms" in this anthology is found in the published correspondence, *Ever Thine Truly, Love Letters from Sam Houston to Anna Roquet.*

MIRABEAU BUONAPARTE LAMAR led the cavalry at the Battle of San Jacinto and was Houston's vice-president from 1836–1838. As President of the Republic, he obtained recognition from France and Great Britain of Texas independence from Mexico. He moved the capital to Austin. A native of Georgia, Lamar went on to serve in the U.S. Army during the War with Mexico. From 1857 to 1859, he was the American minister to Nicaragua. And he wrote poetry everywhere he went. His body of work is best collected in *The Life and Poems of Mirabeau B. Lamar.* Lamar's efforts to fund colleges by way of land grants gave him the historical nickname of "The Father of Texas Education." Lamar's words, "A cultivated mind is the guardian genius of democracy" are now the motto of the University of Texas at Austin.

JIM LINEBARGER, a native of Abilene, Texas, graduated from high school in Midland before going to Columbia on a football scholarship. The retired professor, a former teacher of creative writing at North Texas University, has published several poetry collections, among them, *Texas Blues and Other Poems, Anecdotal Evidence, The Worchester, Poems,* and *Five Faces.* Jim Linebarger now lives with his wife part of the year in Texas and part in North Carolina.

PAT LITTLEDOG, a native of College Station, has been a bookstore owner, small press publisher, and college professor. She is a versatile writer who is a member of the Texas Institute of Letters. Her critically acclaimed novel, *Afoot in a Field of Men and Other Stories from Dallas' East Side,* was reprinted by Atlantic Monthly Press. Among her other books are *The God Chaser; In Search of the Holy Mother of Jobs;* and the award-winning *Border Healing Woman: The Story of Jewel Babb.* Ms. LittleDog, continues to write book reviews and short stories, while living on a farm in Caldwell County where she raises goats and other livestock.

JANET LOWERY is a professor at the University of Saint Thomas in Houston. Her poems have appeared in national literary journals as well as in anthologies. In 2007, Lowery's play, *Traffic in Women,* was staged at the Jones Theatre in Houston.

PEGGY ZULEIKA LYNCH has had her poems published in *Touchstone, Texas in Poetry,* and *Sulphur River Review.* With her late husband Edmund C. Lynch, she co-edited the anthology, *Of Hide and Horn: A Sesquicentennial Anthology of Texas Poems.* Among her book-length collections are *Stacks and Tiles, Ups and Downs,* and *Gandy Dancers.* The University of Texas graduate, who is also known for her work in promoting Texas culture, lives in San Antonio.

WALTER MCDONALD was the 2001 Texas Poet Laureate. A professor of creative writing retired from Texas Tech University, McDonald has won six Texas Institute of Letters awards, including the Lon Tinkle Award for Career Excellence. In addition, the prolific poet has received four National Cowboy Hall of Fame Western Heritage Awards, and his poetry has been read on NPR. Some of his books are *All Occasions, Blessings the Body Gave, The Flying Dutchman, Rafting the Brazos, After the Noise of Saigon, Night Landings, Great Lonely Places of the Texas Plains, Where the Skies Are Not Cloudy,* and *All That Matters: The Texas Plains in Photographs and Poems.* The native West Texan's most recent collection is *Faith Is A Radical Master: New and Selected Poems.*

NJOKI MCELROY, playwright, folklorist, poet, and teacher, is on the faculties of Northwestern and Southern Methodist Universities. She has had twelve plays produced with her poetry and fiction. McElroy is founder of the Cultural Workshop of North Chicago and the Back Home With the Folks Festival in Dallas. "The Porch Gatherers" is excerpted from *Fruits of the Spirit,* a memoir in progress.

LARRY MCMURTRY has won an Oscar, a National Book award, and a Pulitzer. His masterful novels include *The Last Picture Show, Terms of Endearment,* and *Lonesome Dove.* Don Graham places his novels among the best of American letters: "Larry McMurtry's *Lonesome Dove,* a glorious, gritty epic of the trail-drive era, stands first among Westerns and rivals classics such as *Moby Dick.*" McMurtry's nonfiction studies are *In a Narrow Grave: Essays on Texas, Flim Flam: Essay on Hollywood, Walter Benjamin at the Dairy Queen, Roads, Crazy Horse, Paradise,* and *Sacajawea's Nickname: Essays on the American West.* His nonfiction and fiction together interpret the last days of the West, as does "For Erwin Smith, Cowboy Photographer" in this book. With Dianna Ossana, he co-wrote *Pretty Boy Floyd* and *Zeke and Ned,* and co-edited the anthology, *Still Wild: A Collection of Western Stories.* McMurtry's more recent works of fiction include his four *Berrybender* novels and *Telegraph Days: A Novel.* As a college student McMurtry wrote poetry. The native Texan and part-time resident of Archer City once served as President of PEN International.

JAS. MARDIS, poet, is known for his social and literary commentary. Mardis, who lives in Dallas, received the 2000 Pushcart Prize in poetry for his "Invisible Man." Mardis edited the anthology, *KenteCloth: Southwest Voices of the African Diaspora* (1998). His collections are *Southern Tongue, Hanging Time,* and *The Ticking and the Time Going Past.* He has had individual poems appear in *New Texas, Texas in Poetry, !TEX!,* and in *Pushcart.*

VAIDA STEWART MONTGOMERY was born in the Texas Panhandle in 1888 and as a child survived the frontier with her family in a clay dugout. In 1948, she won a Texas Institute of Letters poetry award for *Hail for Rain.* With their Kaleidograph Press, she and her husband Whitney Montgomery produced some fifty books that are a lasting contribution to state literature.

WHITNEY MONTGOMERY, was born in Navarro County in 1877, and worked on his family farm before moving to Dallas. His poetry books are *Joseph's Coat, Corn Silks and Cotton Blossoms, Brown Fields and Bright Lights,* and *Hounds in the Hills.* Whitney Montgomery helped establish the Poetry Society of Texas and was President of the Texas Institute of Letters.

MICHAEL A. MOORE has been teaching and writing haiku since 1990. Moore has published anthologies of haiku with his Mustard Seed Press. A former resident of San Antonio, he now resides in the Dallas area. He currently teaches haiku in schools, K-12, and in colleges throughout Texas. His collections of the Japanese art form include *Haiku Landscapes, Chocolate Chips: Contemporary Haiku,* and *Vista Contemporanea de Haiku.*

JACK E. MURPHY was a successful Dallas businessman whose zeal for life can be seen his poetry. His formal education began in a one-room rural school in Grayson County and finished in graduate school at Harvard University. He served as President of the Poetry Society of Texas. His collections are *Where Rainbows Wait* and *The West Side of the Mountain.*

JACK MYERS is director of creative writing at Southern Methodist University. He is the author of seven volumes of poetry, *The Family War, Blindsided,* and *One On One,* to name three. He is the co-author of *The Dictionary of Poetic Terms,* a University of North Texas Press book, and he edited the anthology, *New American Poets of the 90s.* Jack Myer's 1986 *As Long As You're Happy,* was winner of a National Poetry Series award, selected by Nobel Laureate Seamus Heaney. The Massachusetts native has been awarded two NEA fellowships and two Texas Institute of Letters honors. Jack Myers was 2003 Poet Laureate of Texas.

BERTA HART NANCE was born near Albany, Texas, in 1883. Nance's father ran a store near the walls of Fort Griffin where Berta Hart Nance grew up amid the closing of the Western frontier. She was a short story writer and poet. In the 1930s, many Texas teachers assigned Nance's "Cattle" for recitation in classrooms. Her line, "Other states were carved or born, Texas grew from hide and horn" is still remembered today.

ISABEL NATHANIEL, a native New Yorker, came to Dallas to marry author Bryan Woolley. Her *The Dominion of Lights* received the 1997 Texas Institute of Letters Award for the Best Book of Poetry, and other honors include a *Discovery/The Nation* prize, five Poetry Society of America awards, and *Southwest Review's* McGinnis-Ritchie Award. Her poems have been published in *Poetry, The Nation, Ploughshares, Texas Observer, Southern Poetry Review.* Others poems and have been anthologized in *Texas in Poetry 2, Ravishing DisUnities, Best Texas Writing,* and *Poetry in Motion from Coast to Coast.*

VIOLETTE NEWTON in her ninth decade writes and publishes fiction and poetry. Among her books of poetry are *The Proxy, Scandal and Other Poems,* and *The Shamrock Cross.* Her writings have appeared in various anthologies, including *Travois, Texas Stories and Poems, New Texas 92,* and *Texas Short Stories 2.* The Texas Poet Laureate, 1973–1974, Ms. Newton has long lived in Beaumont.

NAOMI SHIHAB NYE, editor, teacher, and poet lives in San Antonio. She has received two Texas Institute of Letters awards for *Different Ways to Pray* and *Hugging the Jukebox,* the latter also earning a National Poetry series award. In 2002, Bill Moyers in his PBS series *Now* interviewed Ms. Nye, helping her gain a national readership. She is the recipient of a Guggenheim Fellowship and four Pushcarts. The Palestinian-American has also edited popular anthologies, among them *This Tree Older Than You Are, The Space Between Our Footsteps, Is This Forever, Or What?: Poems & Paintings from Texas,* and *This Same Sky,* this last being selected as a Notable Book by the American Library Association.

DAVE OLIPHANT was born in Fort Worth, attended high school in Beaumont, and now lives outside Austin. With Prickly Pear Press, Oliphant published many writers, early in their career. Oliphant edited the anthologies *Washing The Cow's Skull: Lavando La Calavera De Vaca* and *Texas Roundup.* His own prose and poetry embraces a diversity of subjects with books that include *On a High Horse: Views Mostly of Latin American* and *Texan Poetry, Maria's Poems, The Early Swing Era: 1930 to 1941,* and *Memories of Texas Towns.* He has out two new books, a translation from a Chilean poet, and a third study on Texas music.

CLAIRE OTTENSTEIN-ROSS has had her poetry anthologized as well as published in literary journals and yearbooks. The editor, publisher, and poet co-wrote, with Violette Newton, *Because We Dream* and edited the anthology, *Texas Rib-Ticklers: An Anthology of Humorous Poems by Texas Poets.* Among her book-length poetry collections are *In the Shadow of His Wings* and *Shared Blessings: Poems of Inspirations.* She lives in Texas near the Louisiana border.

BONNIE PARKER was born in Rowena in Central Texas in 1910. After her father died, her family moved to West Dallas, looking for a better life. In high school, Parker was an honor student who had a gift for writing poetry noted by her English teacher. One of her poems, not in *A Students' Treasury of Texas Poetry* can be found on her tombstone. At twenty, she met Clyde Barrow and soon joined the Barrow Gang. The folkloric couple as told in books, music, and movies died in a notorious ambush in 1934.

ROBERT PHILLIPS lives with his wife Judith in Houston. His national honors include an Award in Literature from the American Academy of Arts and a Pushcart Prize and recently, one of his poetry books was nominated for a Pulitzer Prize. The University of Houston teacher of creative writing is author of seven full length-books of poetry and three books of short fiction. Phillips's poetry collection, *Breedown Lane,* was named a Notable Book of the Year by the *New York Times Book Review.* Robert Phillips's recent titles include *Circumstances Beyond Our Control* and *Spinach Days.*

CAROL COFFEE REPOSA is a professor at San Antonio College and career poet. Twice nominated for Pushcart prizes, she has received two Fulbright/Hays Fellowships. Her poetry has appeared in *Concho River Review, Blue Mesa Review,* and *The Formalist.* Carol Coffee Reposa's books of poetry are *At the Border: Winter Lights* (1995), *The Green Room* (1998), and *Facts of Life* (2002).

GRACE ROSS was a native West Texan who contributed to regional literary anthologies and yearbooks. In the 1940s and 1950s, Grace Ross served as an officer of both the Fort Worth Poetry Club and the Poetry Society of Texas.

RICHARD SALE, as a child with his parents, followed the oilfields around Texas. He became the editor and publisher of Trilobite Press as well as the editor of the journal *Texas Books in Review.* Sale was a Fulbright Lecturer in American Civilization and Literature in Morocco in 1963–1964. He is Professor Emeritus, University of North Texas. Sale has authored five books of poetry, including *The Return of the Sundance Kid, Dime Western, The Tortilla of Heaven, Curing Susto.* His most recent, *Freeze and Thaw,* was released in 2006.

LEWIS SALINAS, a Texas native, grew up in the Dallas suburb of Oak Cliff. He has published his reviews and poetry in Texas and California newspapers and literary magazines. At present, he is an MFA student in Los Angeles.

ARTHUR M. SAMPLEY was born in Leander and received his doctorate at the University of Texas at Austin in 1930. Sampley taught at Sul Ross State Teachers College before he joined the English Department faculty of North Texas State University. However, his love of the Big Bend area stayed with him long after he had transferred to Denton.

His poem in *A Students' Treasury of Texas Poetry,* "South Rim: Big Bend National Park," recaptures the area's majesty. His poetry collections earned awards from the Texas Institute of Letters in 1947 and 1951. The Poet Laureate of Texas, 1951–1953, once said that his best critic was his wife Vera, who always improved his revisions.

JAN EPTON SEALE writes short fiction, creative nonfiction, and poetry. Critics Sylvia Ann Grider and Lou Halsell Rodenberger called Seale "one of Texas's most versatile writers." Seale's stories and poetry have aired on National Public Radio. Among Jan Epton Seale's body of work are the nonfiction *The Nuts-&Bolts Guide to Writing Your Life Story* and *Valley Ark: Life Along the Rio* (with Ansen Seale), short story collection, *Airlift,* the poetry collections, *Bonds, Sharing the House, The Yin of It,* and *The Wonder Is: New and Selected Poems, 1974–2004.* She has a poem in the newly released anthology, *What Wildness Is This: Women Write about the Southwest.* Jan Epton Seale lives with her husband Carl in the Rio Grande Valley.

MARTIN STAPLES SHOCKLEY, born in Virginia, became Distinguished Professor at North Texas State University in Denton. He served as a President of the Texas Folklore Society and the Poetry Society of Texas and was a member of the Texas Institute of Letters. Along with books of literary criticism, he edited the landmark anthology, *Southwest Writers Anthology* (1967), which contains selections from both J. Frank Dobie and Larry McMurtry. Martin Shockley's retrospective collection of prose and poetry is *Last Roundup* (1994).

Cecil Eugene Shuford, known as **GENE SHUFORD**, served in World War II in the Air Force as a ground school flight instructor. After being a reporter, he became the department head of journalism at North Texas State University. Editors selected his work for inclusion in *Southwest Review, Saturday Evening Post, Kenyon Review, Scribners,* and *New York Times.* Among Shuford's collections are *The Red Bull, 1300 Main Street and Other Poems, Flowering Noose,* and *Selected Poems,* the last title receiving the 1972 Texas Institute of Award for Poetry.

MARCELLA SIEGEL, who wrote the poetry book, *Swift Season* (1987), is remembered in poetry circles for serving as President of Southwest Writers and as that of the Poetry Society of Texas. She saw her work published in *Christian Science Monitor* and *The Saturday Evening Post.*

NAOMI STROUD SIMMONS is a native of Amarillo. As a child, she survived the dust storms of the 1930s. Her poem, "Black Sunday, April 14, 1935" comes from personal memory. Naomi Stroud Simmons's work has been included in *Grasslands Review, New Texas 2001,* and *Is This Forever, Or What?* She teaches poetry in Fort Worth area schools.

GOLDIE CAPERS SMITH was educated in the public schools of Dallas and attended Southern Methodist University. The longtime Corpus Christi journalist wrote the scholarly *Creative Arts in Texas* (1926), which recorded Texas culture of her day. Among her six books of poetry are *Swords of Laughter* (1932) and *Deep in the Furrow* (1950).

RED STEAGALL has a following as a musician, songwriter, TV personality, and poet. He is a recognized authority on Texas cattle culture. And Red Steagall is a real cowboy, if one with a college degree. His body of work includes *Ride for the Brand, Born to This Land: Poems by Red Steagall and Photographs by Skeeter Hagler,* and recently *Red Steagall: New and Selected Works.* He has to his credits National Cowboy and Western Heritage Museum awards. The native Texan served as the 2006 Texas Poet Laureate.

PAT STODGHILL was a five-time President of the Poetry Society of Texas as well as President of the National Federation of State Poetry Societies. Her pieces have been published in *Of Hide and Horn, Texas in Poetry,* and *New Texas 92.* Stodghill has taught at Southern Methodist University and lives in Dallas. Her collections include *Mirror Images* and *Kaleidoscope Pieces.* She served as the 1978–1979 Texas Poet Laureate.

CARMEN TAFOLLA has authored five books of poetry, one volume of non-fiction, seven screenplays, and numerous short stories, articles and children's works. She wrote the nonfiction study in racism, *To Split a Human: Mitos, Machos y la Mujer Chicana.* Her book of poetry, *Sonnets to Human Beings,* received First Prize in Poetry of the UCI National Literary Competition. Her prose and poetry was been anthologized in *New Growth 2, Texas Short Stories 2,* and *!TEX!,* as well as in a number of American literature textbooks adopted for elementary and high schools. Carmen Tafolla's recent releases include the children's book, *Baby Coyote and the Old Woman / El Coyotito y la Viejita* and the poetry collection, *Sonnets and Salsa.* The author and her husband Ernesto Bernal live in San Antonio.

CHUCK TAYLOR edited Cedar Rock and Slough Press, two notable publishing houses that contributed to state literature. Taylor's short story collections include *The Lights of the City: Stories from Austin* (1984) and *Drifter's Story* (1986). Among the titles of his poetry books are *Ordinary Life* (1984), and *Flying (A Primer)* (2004). His collections include, *What Do You Want, Blood?,* which received an Austin Book Award. He is a Texas A&M professor of creative writing and has published his prose and poetry in *Concho River Review, Texas Quarterly,* and in other literary magazines. His most recent book of poetry is *Heterosexual: A Love Story.*

LARRY D. THOMAS of Houston is the 2008 Poet Laureate of Texas. The Houstonian has published five collections of poetry and has a collection forthcoming from TCU Press. In 1998, he retired from his probation officer day job, becoming a full-time poet. Among his other honors are the 2004 Violet Crown Award, 2003 Western Heritage Award, and two Pushcart Prize nominations. Thomas's most recent book is *Stark Beauty,* and *The Fraternity of Oblivion,* is also forthcoming.

JAS. D. THORN worked as a lawyer and was a member of the Barrington Fiction Club, a Dallas literary critique group. "The Sigh of the Old Cattlemen," first appeared in the 1936 anthology, *The Fountain Unsealed.*

FREDERICK TURNER, Oxford graduate, Shakespeare scholar, science-fiction novelist, and poet, was born in Northamptonshire, England in 1943. The professor and scholar became a citizen of the United States in 1977 and now is a professor of creative writing at the University of Texas at Dallas. Turner's publications include *Shakespeare's Romeo* *and Juliet, Essays on Literature and Science, April's Winds,* and *Essays on Literature and Science.* He has appeared on two PBS documentaries, "The Elephant on the Hill" and "The Web of Life." In 2006, his play, *The Prayers of Dallas,* was performed. He lives with his wife, Mei Lin, in Richardson.

MARY VANEK lives in Amarillo, not currently working in academia. She has received a grant from the MacDowell Artists' Colony, and her poetry has appeared in *Concho River Review, Bloomsbury Review,* and *American Literary Review.*

WILLIAM ALLEN WARD was born in Corsicana. The career journalist had by-lines in the newspapers in El Paso, Fort Worth, and Dallas. He began writing poetry while in the Pacific during World War II, where he reported as a correspondent for the *El Paso Times.* He is typical of many gifted Texas writers who made a living as a teacher or a journalist while crafting poetry on the side. I took "Texas" from the 1934 anthology, *New Voices of the Southwest.*

CHRIS WILLERTON, a native of Borger, achieved a black belt in karate and is the Honors Program Director at Abilene Christian University. Willerton has directed the Texas Reading Circuit and worked with the Texas Commission on the Arts. His poetry has appeared in *Southern Poetry Review, Concho River Review, Tar River Poetry,* and in other journals and anthologies. Not unlike the narrator of "Our Speaker This Morning," he is an invited speaker at churches around Abilene. Recently, Chris Willerton published the critical study, *The Waltz He Was Born For: An Introduction to the Writing of Walt McDonald.*

DAVID C. YATES founded *Cedar Rock Literary Magazine* and Cedar Rock Press, a historical example of what an editor and publisher of a small press can accomplish. His poem, "Washing the Cow's Skull," is the title poem of the Dave Oliphant anthology. Yates's books of poetry are *Making Bread, Motions* and *Riding for the Dome.* He is fondly remembered as a Texas poet with a voice of his own.

FAY YAUGER lived in Wichita Falls. From the 1930s into the 1950s many American lovers of poetry followed her work. J. Frank Dobie, the foremost scholar of Southwestern literature, highly ranked a Yauger poem: "At the top of all I should place Fay Yauger's 'Planter's Charm,' published in a volume of the same title."

Attributions for the poets, other than personal correspondence and online biographies:

Christensen, Paul. *West of the American Dream: An Encounter with Texas.* College Station: Texas A&M University Press. 2001.

Dobie, J. Frank. *Guide to Life and Literature of the Southwest.* Second Printing. Dallas: Southern Methodist University Press. 1958.

Edwards, Margaret *Royalty. Poet Laureate of Texas: 1932–1966.* Second Printing. San Antonio: The Naylor Company. 1966.

Graham, Don. *Lone Star Literature: from the Red River to the Rio Grande.* New York: W.W. Norton. 2003.

Grider, Sylvia Ann and Lou Halsell Rodenberger. *Texas Women Writers: A Tradition of Their Own.* College Station: Texas A&M University Press. 1997.

Lee, James Ward. *Adventures with a Texas Humanist.* TCU Press. 2004.

Pilkington, Tom. *State of Mind: Texas Literature and Culture.* College Station: Texas A&M University Press. 1998.

Treherne, John. *The Strange History of Bonnie and Clyde.* New York: Stein and Day. 1984.

Tyler, Ron et al., *The New Handbook of Texas: In Six Volumes.* Austin: The Texas State Historical Association. 1996.

Specific entries used in *A Students' Treasury of Texas Poetry* are "Karle Wilson Baker" by Edwin W. Gaston, Jr., "William Laurence Chittenden" by Shay Bennett, "Grace Noll Crowell" by Betty S. Flowers, "Mary Austin Holley" by Curtis B. Dall, "Boyce B. House" by Harry P. Hewin, "Samuel Houston" by Thomas H. Kreneck, "Mirabeau Buonaparte Lamar" by Herbert Cambrell, "Berta Hart Nance" by Walter N. Vernon, "Literature" by Don Graham, "Bonnie Parker" by Kristi Strickland, and "Poet Laureate" by Margaret Royalty Edwards.

WORKS CITED

Acosta, Teresa Palomo. "For Maximo Palomo," *Passing Time* and *Texas in Poetry 2* (TCU Press); "Tia Maria," *In the Season of Change* (Eakin Press); "Dangereaux avril," *Nile and Other Poems: A 1985-1994 Notebook, Texas in Poetry: A 150-Year-Anthology* (Center for Texas Studies), and *Texas in Poetry 2;* "Spell my name," *In the Season of Change.*

Baker, Karle Wilson. "Austin" and "Nacogdoches Speaks," *Dreamers on Horseback* (Southwest Press), *Texas in Poetry,* and *Texas in Poetry 2.*

Barney, William D. "A Ballad for Bill Pickett," *A Cowtown Chronicle* (Browder Springs Press) and *Texas in Poetry 2;* "Mr. Bloomer's Birds," *A Part of Space: Ten Texas Writers* (TCU Press), *The Killdeer Crying* (Prickly Pear Press), *Texas in Poetry,* and *Texas in Poetry 2;* "A Rufous-Crowned Sparrow Seen Loitering Below Possum Kingdom Dam," *A Part of Space, The Killdeer Crying, Texas in Poetry,* and *Texas in Poetry 2;* "Mr. Watts and the Whirlwind," *A Cowtown Chronicle* and *Texas in Poetry 2;* "Long Gone To Texas," *Long Gone To Texas* (Nortex Press), *Texas in Poetry,* and *Texas in Poetry 2.*

Bateman, Preston P. "Our Centennial!" *Texas Poems* (The Naylor Company) and *Texas in Poetry.*

Birkelbach, Alan. "Coronado Points," *Weighed in the Balance* (Plain View Press) and *Texas in Poetry 2,* and *Alan Birkelbach: New and Selected Poems* (TCU Press); "Event, Clarity," *Weighed in the Balance* and *Alan Birkelbach, New and Selected Poems.*

Boswell, Margie B. "Girls of the Rodeo," *Out Where the West Begins: A Collection of Poems by Forth Worth Authors* (The Kaleidograph Press).

Bradley, Jerry. "How the Big Thicket Got Smaller," *Newsletter Inago, Simple Versions of Disaster* (University of North Texas Press), and *Texas in Poetry 2.*

bridgforth, sharon. Previously unpublished.

Bright, Susan. "Riding the Currents," *Breathing Under Water* (Plainview Press) and *Texas in Poetry 2;* "Makes Them Wild," *Behold Texas: The Poet's View* (Eakin Press), *Texas in Poetry,* and *Texas in Poetry 2.*

Chittenden, Lawrence. "Ennui," *Ranch Verses* (G.P. Putnam's Sons), *Texas in Poetry,* and *Texas in Poetry 2.* "To a Dallas Lady," *Ranch Verses.*

Christensen, Paul. "Summer Nights," *Texas in Poetry* and *Texas in Poetry 2;* "Houston: An Ode (Prolog)," *Signs of the Whelming* (Latitudes Press), *Texas in Poetry* and *Texas in Poetry 2;* "Driving Toward Houston," *Southwestern American Literature, Texas in Poetry 2,* and *Ecotropic Works* (Ecotropic).

Cody, James Marion. "Whooping Crane," *My Body Is a Flute* (Place of Herons Press), *Return*

(Place of Herons Press), and *Texas in Poetry 2;* "Big Thicket Words," *Return* and *Texas in Poetry 2.*

Colquitt, Betsy Feagan. "Duet," New Texas 98 (University of Mary Hardin-Baylor), *Eve— from the Autobiography and Other Poems* (TCU Press), *Texas in Poetry,* and *Texas in Poetry 2.*

Cortez, Sarah. Previously unpublished.

Crack, Jim. *The Texas State Gazette* and *Early Texas Verse: Collected from the Original Newspapers of Texas before 1850* (The Steck Company).

Crouch, A.L. "Mirabeau B. Lamar," *Out Where the West Begins, Texas in Poetry,* and *Texas in Poetry 2.*

Crowell, Grace Noll. "Wagons at Dust," *A Book of the Year 1938* (The Poetry Society of Texas) and *Texas in Poetry;* "Summer Nights in Texas," *Flame in the Wind* (The Southwest Press), *Bright Destiny* (Tardy Publishing Company), *Texas in Poetry,* and *Texas in Poetry 2.*

Crowell, Norman H. "Texas Trails," *Moon in the Steeple* (The Kaleidograph Press) and *Texas in Poetry 2.*

Davis, William V. "Texas: Sesquicentennial," *Descant, Texas in Poetry,* and *Texas in Poetry 2.* "Winter in Texas," *Southwestern American Literature.*

Elizabeth, Martha. "On the Porch—Denton, Texas," *Texas in Poetry* and *Texas in Poetry 2.*

Fink, Robert A. "The Certified Public Accountant Recalls the Early 1950s," *The Ghostly Hitchhiker* (Corona Press) and *Texas in Poetry 2;* "Drought: Sure Signs in Merkle, Texas," *Country Journal, The Ghostly Hitchhiker, Texas in Poetry,* and *Texas in Poetry 2;* "Abilene, TX: We Pull Out For New England," *Descant, Texas in Poetry,* and *Texas in Poetry 2;* "Mesquite," *Poetry, The Ghostly Hitchhiker,* and *Texas in Poetry.*

Fromholz, Steven. "If I Couldn't Get To The River"; Paga Me Publishing (ASCAP) Recording: CD - "Guest In Your Heart" - Felicity Records, 2000; CD - "Live At Anderson Fair" - Felkicity Records, 2001.

Garcia, Edward H. Previously unpublished.

Haddad, Marian. Previously unpublished.

Harrigan, Stephen. "Pecos Bill In Decline," *Sleepyhead* (Calliope Press), *Washing the Cow's Skull* (Prickly Pear Press), *Texas in Poetry,* and *Texas in Poetry 2.*

Hill, Clyde Walton. "The Little Towns of Texas," *The Buccaneer, A Book of the Year 1924* (The Poetry Society of Texas), and *Shining Trails* (Kaleidograph Press), *Texas in Poetry,* and *Texas in Poetry 2.*

Hinojosa-Smith, Rolando. "The Eighth Army at the Chongchon," *Korean Love Songs,* (Justa Editorial), *Texas in Poetry,* and *Texas in Poetry 2;* "Rest Due And Taken," *Korean Love Songs, Texas in Poetry,* and *Texas in Poetry 2.*

Hoggard, James. "Anniversary Trip," *Medea in Taos* (Pecan Grove Press) and *Texas in Poetry 2;* "November," *Texas Observer, Texas in Poetry, Texas in Poetry 2,* and *Wearing the River* (Wings Press).

Holley, Mary Austin. "The Plea of Texas," *The Red-Lander, Early Texas Verse, Texas in Poetry,* and *Texas in Poetry 2.*

House, Boyce. "Texas Poets," *Texas Rhythm and Other Poems* (The Naylor Company);"A Mocking-bird," *Blue Moon, Texas Rhythm and Other Poems,* and *Texas in Poetry 2.*

Houston, Margaret Bell (Belle). "The Old Oak Speaks," *Lanterns in the Dusk* (Vail-Ballou Press), *The Singing Heart and Other Poems* (Cokesbury Press), *Texas in Poetry,* and *Texas in Poetry 2;* "Cerelle," *Lanterns in the Dusk* and *New Voices of the Southwest* (Tardy Publishing Company).

Houston, Sam. "Texian Call to Arms," *Ever Thine Truly: Love Letters from Sam Houston to Anna Raquet* (Jenkins Garrett Press) and *Texas in Poetry 2.*

Lamar, Mirabeau Buonaparte. "San Jacinto," *Educational Free Press* and *The Life and Poems of Mirabeau B. Lamar* (The University of North Carolina Press), *Texas in Poetry,* and *Texas in Poetry 2.*

Linebarger, Jim. "Oppa," *Southwest Review, The New Breed* (Prickly Pear Press), *Five Faces* (Trilobite Press), *The Texas Anthology* (Sam Houston State University Press), *Texas in Poetry,* and *Texas in Poetry 2;* "Coyote," *Descant, Texas Blues* (Point Rider Press), *Texas in Poetry,* and *Texas in Poetry 2.*

LittleDog, Pat. "cowgirl," *From Hide and Horn: A Sesquicentennial Anthology of Texas Poems* (Eakin Press), *Texas in Poetry,* and *Texas in Poetry 2;* "in austin reigns a bald-headed queen," *Tonics, Teas, Roots, and Remedies* (Slough Press), *Texas in Poetry,* and *Texas in Poetry 2.*

Lowery, Janet. "Texas Splendor," *Texas in Poetry* and *Texas in Poetry 2.*

Lynch, Peggy Zuleika. "A True Texan," *Stacks and Files* (Keyhole Press), *Behold Texas, Texas in Poetry,* and *Texas in Poetry 2.*

McDonald, Walter. "In Fields of Buffalo," *Where Skies Are Not Cloudy* (University of North Texas Press) and *Texas in Poetry 2;* "Riddles Come Clear At Midnight," *Christian Century* and *Faith Is A Radical Master: New and Selected Poems* (Abilene Christian University Press); "Fathers and Sons," *Prairie Schooner* and *Blessings the Body Gave* (Ohio State University Press); "Growing Up Near Escondido Canyon," *Windsor Review* (Canada) and *The Digs at Escondido Canyon* (Texas Tech University Press); "Hawks in a Bitter Blizzard," *The Atlantic, All That Matters: The Texas Plains in Photographs and Poems* (Texas Tech Press), *Texas in Poetry,* and *Texas in Poetry 2;* "Wind and Hardscrabble," *TriQuarterly* and *The Flying Dutchman* (Ohio State University Press), *Texas in Poetry,* and *Texas in Poetry 2;* "Springtime in Texas," *Descant* and *Great Lonely Places of the Texas Plains* (Texas Tech University Press); "After the Random Tornado," *All Occasions* (Notre Dame Press) and *Texas in Poetry 2.* "August on Padre Island," *Sonoma Mandela* and *Rafting the Brazos* (University of North Texas Press); "All the Old Songs," *Where the Skies Are Not Cloudy* (University of North Texas Press), *Texas in Poetry 2,* and *Roundup* (Prickly Pear Press).

McElroy, Njoki. "Present Moments," *Texas in Poetry 2.*

McMurtry, Larry. "For Erwin Smith, Cowboy Photographer," *Southwest Review* and *Texas in Poetry 2.*

Mardis, Jas. "Good-bye Summer," *Southern Tongue* (B-Fest Publications), *Texas in Poetry,* and *Texas in Poetry 2.*

Montgomery, Vaida Stewart. "Cattle Brands," *A Book of the Year 1946* (The Poetry Society of Texas), *Hail for Rain* (The Kaleidograph Press), "To the Rattlesnake," from *Locoed,* Kaleidograph Press, 1930, *Texas in Poetry,* and *Texas in Poetry 2.*

Montgomery, Whitney. "Outlaws," *Hounds in the Hills* (Kaleidograph Press), *Texas in Poetry,* and *Texas in Poetry 2;* "Death Rode a Pinto Pony," *Hounds in the Hills, Southwest Writers Anthology,* (Steck-Vaughn Company) and *Texas in Poetry 2.*

Moore, Michael A. Haiku: Hands shading my eyes and Haiku: Lazy afternoon. Previously unpublished.

Murphy, Jack E. "Heave Me A Mountain, Lord!" *A Book of the Year 1982* (The Poetry Society of Texas), *The West Side of the Mountain* (Nortex Press), *Texas in Poetry,* and *Texas in Poetry 2.*

Myers, Jack. "The Experts," *American Poetry Review, Blindsided* (Godine Publications), *The Glowing River: New and Selected Poems* (Invisible Cities Press), and *Texas in Poetry 2.*

Nance, Berta Hart. "Moonlight," "Old Fort Griffin," and "Cattle," *Flute in the Distance* (Kaleidograph Press), *Texas in Poetry,* and *Texas in Poetry 2.*

Nathaniel, Isabel. "The Weepers" *Field, The Dominion of Lights* (Copper Beach Press), and *Poetry in Texas 2;* "On the Patio, Dallas," *The Texas Observer, The Dominion of Lights,* and *Poetry in Motion from Coast to Coast* (Norton).

Newton, Violette. "The Witness, Susanna Dickinson," *This Is A House To Stand* (Newton Notebook), *Texas in Poetry,* and *Texas in Poetry 2;* "Spindletop Evenings," *The Scandal and Other Poems* (Nortex Press); "Texas Poetry," *The Scandal and Other Poems, Texas in Poetry,* and *Texas in Poetry 2;* "A Mythology of Snow," *The Scandal and Other Poems, Texas in Poetry,* and *Texas in Poetry 2.*

Nye, Naomi Shihab. "Site of the Indian Fights of 1871, Abilene," *Southwest: A Contemporary Anthology* (Red Earth Press), *Texas in Poetry,* and *Texas in Poetry 2;* "My Father and the Figtree," *Different Ways to Pray* (Breitenbush Books), *Words Under the Words: Selected Poems* (Far Corner Books), and *Texas in Poetry 2;* "The Little Brother Poem," *Different Ways to Pray, Words Under the Words,* and *Texas in Poetry 2;* "San Antonio Mi Sangre: from the Hard Season," *Fuel* (BOA Editions); "The Endurance of Poth, Texas," *Mint* (State Street Press), *Texas in Poetry,* and *Texas in Poetry 2;* "Going for Peaches, Fredericksburg, Texas," *Yellow Glove* (Breitenbush Books) and *Words Under the Words;* "The Lost Parrot," *Hugging the Jukebox* (E.P. Dutton), *Texas in Poetry, Words Under the Words,* and *Texas in Poetry 2;* "At the Seven-Mile Ranch, Comstock, Texas," *Hugging the Jukebox* (Breitenbush Books), *Texas in Poetry,* and *Words Under the Words.*

Oliphant, Dave. "Dallas," *Lines and Mounds* (Thorp Springs Press), *Memories of Texas Towns & Cities* (Host Publications), *Texas in Poetry,* and *Texas in Poetry 2.*

Ottenstein-Ross, Claire. "The Judge," *A Book of the Year 1995* (The Poetry Society of Texas) and *Texas in Poetry 2.*

Parker, Bonnie. "The Story of Bonnie and Clyde." *Fugitives: The Story of Clyde Barrow and Bonnie Parker: As Told by Bonnie's Mother and Clyde's Sister* (The Ranger Press).

Phillips, Robert. "Texas Tanka," *Texas in Poetry 2.*

Reposa, Carol Coffee. "Hill Country Rest Home," *At the Border: Winter Lights* (Pecan Grove Press); "Dawn in El Paso," *New Texas 98* and *Texas in Poetry 2;* "Alamo Plaza at Night," *Acequía* and *Texas in Poetry 2.*

Ross, Grace. "Oil Well Fire," *Texas Legacy* (Poetry Publisher Press) and *Poetry in Texas 2.*

Sale, Richard. "Stilts and Other Vehicles," *Dime Western* (Chawd Razin), *Travois: An Anthology of Texas Poetry* (Thorp Springs Press), *The Texas Anthology, The Tortilla of Heaven* (University of North Texas Press), *Texas in Poetry,* and *Texas in Poetry 2.*

Salinas, Lewis. "Exhausted by I-35, A Couple Comes Up on the Third Belton-Temple Exit,"; "My Three Uncles," previously unpublished.

Sampley, Arthur M. "South Rim: Big Bend National Park," *A Book of the Year 1948* and *Furrow with Blackbirds* (Kaleidograph Press) and *Arthur M Sampley: Selected Poems 1937-1971* (North Texas State University Press).

Seale, Jan Epton. "Hill Country Bird Woman," *The Wonder Is* (Panther Creek Press); "Big Bend: Lion Warning," *New Texas 2000, Texas in Poetry 2;* "And these signs shall follow them that believe," *The Wonder Is.*

Shockley, Martin S. "Armadillo," *Southwest Writers Anthology, Round-Up* (Center for Texas Studies), *Texas in Poetry,* and *Texas in Poetry 2.*

Shuford, Gene. "The Visit" from "The Death in Our Family," *Gene Shuford: Selected Poems 1933-1971* (North Texas State University Press), *Texas in Poetry,* and *Texas in Poetry 2;* "The Horse in My Yard," *A Book of the Year 1969, Selected Poems, Texas in Poetry,* and *Texas in Poetry 2.*

Siegel, Marcella. "Waiting Wife," *A Book of the Year 1981* (The Poetry Society of Texas), *Swift Season* (Nortex Press), *Texas in Poetry,* and *Texas in Poetry 2.*

Simmons, Naomi Stroud. "Black Sunday, April 14, 1935" *A Book of the Year 1996* (The Poetry Society of Texas) and *Texas in Poetry 2.*

Smith, Goldie Capers. "Ballad of a Bombardier from Texas," *A Book of the Year 1944-45* (The Poetry Society of Texas), *Deep in This Furrow* (Kaleidograph Press), *Texas in Poetry,* and *Texas in Poetry 2.*

Steagall, Red. "The Memories in Grandmother's Trunk," *Ride for the Brand* (Bunkhouse Press) and *Red Steagall: New and Selected Poems* (TCU Press); "The Real America," *The Fence That Me and Shorty Built* (Bunkhouse Press) and *Red Steagall: New and Selected Poems.*

Stodghill, Pat. "Traitor (Sam Houston—1857)," *Mirrored Images* (Nortex Press), *Texas in Poetry,* and *Texas in Poetry 2;* "Rattlesnake Roundup," *A Texas Book of the Year 1970* (The Poetry Society of Texas), *Mirrored Images, Texas in Poetry,* and *Texas in Poetry 2.*

Tafolla, Carmen. "Mission San José," *Sonnets to Human Beings* (Lalo Press), *Texas in Poetry, Texas in Poetry 2,* and *Sonnets and Salsa* (Wings Press); "This River Here," *Texas in Poetry 2, Sonnets and Salsa,* and *Roundup;* "Mi Tia Sofía," *Sonnets to Human Beings,*

Travois, *Texas in Poetry*, and *Texas in Poetry 2;* "Health Care," *Sonnets and Salsa.* "Aquí," *Sonnets to Human Beings* and *Texas in Poetry 2.*

Taylor, Chuck. "Poem to Ma Ferguson," *From Hide and Horn*, *Texas in Poetry*, and *Texas in Poetry 2;* "our texas economy," *Concho River Review*, *What Do You Want, Blood?* (Slough Press), *Texas in Poetry*, and *Texas in Poetry 2.*

Thomas, Larry D. "Caddoan Indian Mound," *The Texas Review;* "The Great Storm," *Texas in Poetry 2;* "January Lull," previously unpublished; "Kudzu," previously unpublished; "Palo Duro Canyon," Sulphur River Review.

Thorn, Jas. D. "The Sigh of the Old Cattleman," *The Fountain Unsealed* (Clyde C. Cockrell Company) and *Texas in Poetry 2.*

Turner, Frederick. "The Poet Gets Drowsy on the Road," *Texas in Poetry 2:* "Early Warning," *Southwest Review* and *Texas in Poetry 2.* "110 Degrees in Dallas," *Texas in Poetry 2.*

Vanek, Mary. "Summer Begins Outside Dalhart, Texas," *Concho River Review*, *Texas in Poetry*, and *Texas in Poetry 2.*

Ward, William Allen. "Texas," *New Voices of the Southwest* and *Texas in Poetry 2.*

Willerton, Chris. "Battle of Adobe Walls" *From Hide and Horn*, *Texas in Poetry*, and *Texas in Poetry 2;* "Our Speaker This Morning," *Kansas Quarterly* and *Texas in Poetry 2.*

Yates, David C. "Sunset Along U.S. Highway 90 Between Langtry and Sanderson," *Riding for the Dome* (Cedar Rock Press), *Texas in Poetry*, and *Texas in Poetry 2;* "Washing the Cow's Skull," *Motions* (Lattitudes Press), *Washing the Cow's Skull*, *Texas in Poetry*, and *Texas in Poetry 2.*

Yauger, Fay. "I Remember" and "County Fair," *Planter's Charm* (Kaleidograph Press), *Texas in Poetry*, and *Texas in Poetry 2.*

ACKNOWLEDGMENTS

I BEGIN CREDITS with persons in the past, those originated or played on my curiosity about my native state and later, my interest in poetry: my parents, Robert Nelson Hill and Julia Giddens Hill, along with my grandmothers who read poems to me. I must mention my enthusiastic seventh-grade Texas history teacher, Marguerite McDade as well as my sui generis graduate school professor, A.C. Greene.

I would then credit a number of souls yet among the quick: Don Graham, Paul Kenneth Oswalt, Margie West, Michael Hennech, Clay Reynolds, James Gilbert Clarke, Judy Alter, Susan R. Petty, Melinda Esco, Thomas Edward Brawner, Martha Penalosa, Betty Wiesepape, Janet McIntosh, Robert Compton, Judyth Rigler, Kent Biffle, Charles Daniel, Terence Dalrymple, Dave Oliphant, Laurie Champion, Russ Teeter, Thea Temple, Jack Myers, Richard Sale, and James Ward Lee.

PHOTO CREDITS

Carmen Tafolla. *Photo credit: Courtesy of Scott-Foresman*
Naomi Shibab Nye. *Photo credit: Michael Nye.*
William D. Barney. *Photo courtesy of Winston Barney.*

I

INDEX